Sons Of Abraham

Sons Of Abraham

Dr. Monif M. Matouk

CITIOFBOOKS, INC.
3736 Eubank NE Suite A1
Albuquerque, NM 87111-3579
www.citiofbooks.com

Hotline: 1 (877) 389-2759
Fax: 1 (505) 930-7244

Ordering Information:
Quantity sales. Special discounts are available on quantity purchases by corporations, associations, and others. For details, contact the publisher at the address above.

Printed in the United States of America.

ISBN-13:   Paperback   979-8-89391-367-5
            Hardback   979-8-89391-368-2
            eBook   979-8-89391-369-9

Library of Congress Control Number: 2024920455

I dedicate this book to my first and only love, my wife Nadirah. Who fills my world with love and warmth that comes so readily from her pure heart. And to my children Sarah, Andrew and Mathew, whose integrity and strength make me a very proud father. And to my son in law Viktor whose sweet spirit brought increased joy to our lives. And to my grandson Kristian, my beloved and loyal best friend. And to my precious and joyful granddaughters Victoria, Gabriella and Nicole.

I also dedicate this book to the memory of my father Moussa Matouk who instilled in me pride and assurance of identity and a fighting spirit that does not bow down to injustice. And to my mother Kharma whose love, compassion and prayers are ever-present.

I also dedicate this book to my birthplace Syria, the fertile land where Christianity first sprouted and where civilizations started and flourished. Where different communities lived and built a nation together in harmony and brotherly love. A country that is being torn apart now by different factions and ideologies. Praying and hoping that Syria will overcome the horrors and destruction caused by the enemies of humanity and civilization and blossom again through the blood of its martyrs, the strength of its people and the tenacity of its historical character.

Chapter 1

The sum of a man's life is measured at the time of his death. He lay still in his bed watching out of the hospital's window. It was a beautiful blue sky and a warm sunny day. He couldn't see the sun clearly, but its warmth fondled his bare chest, and its rays entered the room through the closed window and tantalized his emotions. He may no longer see the sunshine. Its warm fingers will shortly not be able to pierce the cold earth, or steel and wood in which he will lay, and touch his skin. He knew he was dying. He had a few days, maybe, a few hours to live.

It must be true what they say. At the moment of death, a man's life rolls before his eyes like a film reel. Now, all the different scenes of his life were running quickly before his wandering eyes. Vivid colors, scenes and even sounds. Sounds of laughter and singing. Scenes from his life ran quickly and eagerly before his eyes.

This was Fadi. As he lay in bed he looked much older than he really was. His 54 years of hard living made him look much older than his true age. His eyes, however, had not lost their young and vibrant sparkle. His hair was almost completely gone. He had lost most of his hair at a very early age, and now after his chemotherapy, not much at all was left. Few sparse white hairs around the back and perimeter of his head looked like cactus in a desert. His face was hard and wrinkled. The years of hard work had taken their toll on his skin and his features looked hard as if they were cut from the side of a mountain. His lips were taught and dry. His shoulders were weary but retained their muscle mass. His arms were mostly covered with wires, IV lines and tape. They were bruised and fatigued. His bare chest had several wires placed on it for the heart monitor and a thickened, raised and circular area could be seen underneath the right shoulder where an access port was placed under his skin. He was a man battling for his life. But he was not a beaten man. He was not a fallen soldier. He was a warrior who had fought long and hard on the plains of this battlefield...Life, and now he is finally facing the end of the war.

How far was he now from the place of his birth? He looked out of the window again. He could see the beautiful skies covering Chicago. His adopted home. His true home. The place where he had made his mark in life.

He was very far from the shores of Lebanon now. Far from the place where he first took the air of this world into his newborn lungs. Where he took his first breath and suckled his first meal on this earth. The place where he spent most of his childhood. How much he longed to see it just one more time. To see the places of old. Where he walked and played. The hills he climbed and the fig trees on which branches he spent many hours sitting and watching the sun set on the horizon. The vines that covered the far side of his village like a beautiful oriental rug, well woven and designed. He could almost taste the sweet grapes in his mouth now. He wanted to see his old house, and the path leading from his house into the fields, and the half-broken wall, down from his old house, down where the fields met the prairie, where he first saw her. His first and only love. Layla.

He was 12 years old then. Didn't know much about life or about love. Not that kind of love anyway. He loved his village. He loved waking up in the morning and leaving the warmth of his bed to meet the chilly morning air filled with the smell of milk being warmed up, Tannours being lit up to bake bread, the earth which was covered with a fresh blanket of dew, and he especially loved the smell of orange blossoms in the springtime. He would take several lung fills of air before he even opened his eyes. How he longs to do that just one more time. But that was a world that has completely vanished now.

He loved going to the spring where many of the ladies went early in the day to bring water in their large clay vessels. He wondered how some of these ladies with such small physical statures could carry two or three of these huge vessels that were filled with water and chat and giggle on their way back to their homes as if they were carrying a small load. He loved seeing his mother's face smile with love and adoration as she kissed him in the morning and offered him a fresh loaf of bread with butter smeared all over it and sugar sprinkled over the butter. Oh, he could smell the aroma of the fresh baked bread just coming out of the Tannour right now. And most of all, he loved watching her.

On the day when he first saw her, he was chasing after a lizard that he wanted to catch. He was told by friends that if he ever got into trouble in school and was going to receive punishment, the lizard would come in handy. He only had to smear the blood of a lizard on his hands so that when the teacher hit him on the palms of his hand with that thick wooden stick, he wouldn't feel any pain. Something like that could come in handy indeed. Oh, he wasn't one who got into a lot of trouble, but there were times when he could not keep silent. There were times when somebody was wrongly accused or unjustly punished, and he would not be silent. The teacher would sometimes punish him instead just because of his audacity, but he would not be silent. You can't be silent when wrong is being done. If you don't speak out against it, you would be just as guilty as those who are the perpetrators of injustice. Many times, he spoke out too clearly and too loudly, and his hands suffered the consequences.

On that day he was determined to catch at least one lizard. He would want to keep it alive and feed it until it would be needed. He knew that it would be cruel, but was it also not cruel to be punished for speaking out against injustice.

That morning, he saw the lizard sitting on a rock, taking in the sun shine. He crept up to it but was not fast enough with his cloth bag to catch it. The lizard jumped and ran, and he ran after it. It ran beyond the perimeter of his yard, and down into the fields. He stumbled several times as he ran after it but managed to keep it in his sights. Finally, the lizard got to a broken wall and climbed over it and as he climbed over the wall in pursuit, he fell down on the other side and rolled a couple of times before he came up and looked into the puzzled face of a sweet angle. Blessed lizard. It had led him to a creature that grabbed a hold of his senses and his heart as if he had touched a live wire, and he had done that once when he was visiting the city. Her eyes were so innocent and pure. Her puzzled look so mystifying. Her curly and long strands of hair flew about and gently touched her face as the wind playfully caressed her. He stood there and gazed at her for several moments, then watched a faint smile come over her face as she slowly turned her back to him then ran to the house behind the wall looking back at him once or twice.

He felt very funny then. A sweet sensation of warmth, numbness and tingling that started in his stomach then flooded his entire being as he stood there. He did not want to leave.

That was the first time he saw her. He chased many lizards into her yard after that.

Chapter 2

She tilted her seat back and pulled her jacket tight about her. The tears coming down her cheeks were matched by the huge rain drops falling on her car's windshield. She winced in grief, then broke into deep heavy weeping. She could not imagine life without him. How could life have any meaning whatsoever without his reassuring presence? Without his loving hands running teasingly through her hair. Without those eyes so full of love when he gazed upon her. What meaning would life have without his joyful humor and ever-present laughter? She wished it was her facing death and not him. Oh, how she would gladly trade places with him.

She tried to wipe away her tears. She did not want him to see her cry. She must be brave for him. She knows that her tears are one thing he can't bear. He devoted his life to seeing her happy and to seeing a constant smile on her face. He always lost control of his emotions whenever he saw her crying. He would become lost and confused. Just like a lost baby looking for his mother. She could recognize that glisten in his eyes as he would look at her in wonder and confusion. How despite his great inner strength, he becomes panic stricken whenever she cries.

He was always like that. She remembers long ago after that first day she met him when he suddenly jumped from behind that broken wall into her yard and into her life. She saw him soon after that day by the railroad tracks. She was going with her mother and her aunt to the spring to get water. Her mother had one large clay vessel hugged by her left arm and held closely to her bosom as if it was a child being held closely to her heart. Another vessel was held by her right hand and was dangling down by her side, swinging back and forth with every step as if it was a monkey hanging with one arm from a tree branch and swinging back and forth passing time. The third vessel was held upon her head placed over a thick cloth that was formed like a nest. She always wondered how graceful her mother looked when she was walking down the stony pathway towards the village spring looking ahead as to a distant object, never missing a step or stumbling upon a stone. Never was there such grace as that. Her mother's body moved in perfect motion, hips slightly rotating with each step. Head and shoulders steady as a cedar tree, untethered or shaken by the wind. Her feet dressed in leather sandals glided over the stony pathway as if she was floating on air. They passed the village boundaries and soon came upon the Christian graveyard just east of the village, just before you get to the walnut grove and the spring.

There she saw him leaning upon the trunk of a fig tree crying while looking sorrowfully at something held gently in his hands. She stood for a minute in amazement looking at him. She rarely saw him cry, certainly not without any apparent reason. She pulled on her mother's skirt asking her to stop. Her mother just kept going on her way not disturbed at all by her daughter's prodding.

He held a morning dove in his hands. It was not moving and seemed to be dead. His tears were streaming down his cheeks and dropping into his lap. They passed him by, and he did not lift his head at all. She kept on turning her head as they were going along to watch him, and finally he looked up at her and their eyes met. She saw in his eyes that scared, desperate look that she came to know so well after then. A look she saw in his eyes whenever he saw her crying. His face seemed to change color, and he quickly dropped his eyes. She went away with her mother then walking beside her, going through the motions of the daily morning routine. In her mind though, she could not shake away the picture of the wild haired, freckle-faced, lost looking boy. She wished then that she could sit beside him and share his pain and desperation.

The nurse came in asking him if he needed anything, he said that he was alright and had everything he needed. He never liked attention much. He could take care of himself. He had to do so all his life. His father died when he was very young. He doesn't remember the cause. He doesn't even remember his father very well. Memories of his father were like a silent film with weird unconnected scenes that seemed to run together without purpose. He remembered his father coming back from work in his blue uniform with large spots of sweat covering parts of his chest and underarms. His work boots dirty and dusty with dry soil and mud. A tired look upon his face. Then he remembered his father's ever constant laughter. He remembered him singing with his deep-toned voice while putting his socks on getting ready to go somewhere. And he remembered the loving way in which his father looked at his mother when they talked. Many other scenes that didn't seem to connect or fall together in any discernable pattern. Scenes of his father riding a bicycle, snoring lazily on a stack of hay, fixing things, then, his father lying down in an open coffin eyes closed, lifeless in a new dark suit. His father was never so still before. He was always so full of life, strong, unrelenting. There were also the screams of the women as they pounded on their chests. The wailing pierced his ears and soul. He remembered being utterly still, numb and unable to cry. He suddenly had to face life without his father and life became different, hopeless and complicated.

He heard her footsteps coming down the hallway. They were not any different from other footsteps that he had heard throughout the day, yet he knew. He felt her presence. Felt her tender spirit approaching as she neared the doorway, then suddenly she appeared and he smiled.

It was a wide and full smile that seemed to wash away the pain and fatigue present in his face. It was like a wave that invaded the shore and washed away all the tracks and debris and gave the shore a smooth and clean new face. She cheered:

-How are you feeling today, habibi (my darling)

-Thank God, I am well. I am happy now that you are here.

She held back her tears and pinched herself real hard to maintain her composure,

-I am always with you habibi, if not in body, then in spirit. But I am always with you. Don't you know? We are one.

-I know ya omri (my life) I know that you think of me always. I don't want you to do that, however.. I.. I want you to think of yourself once in a while, you know how important your happiness is to me. I want you to start thinking about life without me. I want you to be realis….

-Don't even finish the words. There is no life without you

-Habibti please, you are my life. As long as you live, I live. As long as you are happy, my spirit rejoices. As long as you are well, my soul will be in peace.

-We will be happy together. We will live, walk and run, eat and drink, labor and rest together. There is no me without you.

-Ya omri please, be reasonable. You should..

-Sh..sh. Stop that now. See what I brought you

-Shourabet Adas (Lentil soup)! Oh.. I love it from your hands. Not even my mother makes it as good as you do. I love anything your hands make, but shourabet adas beats it all.

-Eat ya habibi and be well. I will not leave your side.

Chapter 3

Hazem was on the phone yelling, his voice angry and irritated: Dawod, how can you say that. Our friend needs us now more than ever. Don't do this to him. Your sight will cheer him up.

-Listen Hazem, you know that I can't face him when he is in this shape. You know how emotional I can get. I don't want to weaken his spirit.

-My friend, seeing you will not weaken his spirit, it will elevate his spirit. You know how much we both mean to him and to Layla. We need to be there for them. Now more than ever, they need our support. Look, if I am willing to go and show myself with a bounty on my head, so should you. I am the one who should be worried not you.

-Hazem, I am sorry. You know that. I am just not sure of my reaction when I see him in his death bed like this. You know, I always thought he would go differently. He was such a tremendous soldier.

-I know, I know, but listen, we must go soon. By tomorrow at the latest...

-What about you Hazem. You know that they have placed a bounty on your head. Your family wants you dead for abandoning Islam.

-My family still loves me, Dawod. I am sure of that. It is only that they are under such tremendous pressure from the fanatics. You know that my sister is married to Hassan, one of the Jihadists. He beats her and threatens to divorce her if my family does not execute Al-Ridda law against me.

-What exactly is that law Hazem, and who put it in place?

-It is the law against apostates. If you abandon Islam for any reason, your life is forfeited. Your blood is Halal (religiously permitted) and it is the duty of every Moslem to kill you.

-I can't believe that there are people who still follow such outdated and barbaric practices.

-Oh, you think it is outdated then, let me tell you something: Fanatics are never outdated. They are resistant to change and moderation. Look at how many terrorists are educated in the west, and some have lived in the west for a while. Some have even married western girls. Do they change? No. They become more hardline than ever. They force their western wives to wear Hijab (head dress). They start to grow beards and become more fanatical than Moslems who live in the Middle East. I don't know what happens to them. I guess that they become radicalized in mosques in the west, or they fear losing the religion and believe system that they grew up with, so they cling on to the most extreme form of those believes. Some are doctors and engineers and highly educated people, yet they get led by the Mosque Imams and Sheiks and soon abandon all the values that had led them to come to the west in the first place. Look at the terrorists who drove the airplanes into the two towers. Many of them received their higher education in the west. Back home they react to the way the west supports Israel unconditionally and completely ignores the plight of the Palestinian people. Fanatics don't like differences in opinion. You either think like they do, or you become their enemy. In fact, most people that are killed by Moslem fanatics are Moslems who dare to think or behave more moderately and express more progressive ideas. Look at what happened to Suleiman Rushdi when he spoke about the Satanic Verses. A bounty was immediately placed on his head, and he was declared a Kafer, meaning an infidel, and a Fatwa (religious edict) was given calling for his death.

-What is the story with the Satanic Verses anyway?

-They are verses that are written in the Quran and were spoken by the prophet of Islam praising the idols of Arabia at that time. Moslems say that Satan put these verses into his mouth and he spoke them. Moslem teachers try to hide these verses and don't teach about them. Suleiman Rushdi spoke openly about these verses in his book and they wanted to kill him. They don't want things like that to come to light. It brings the controversial parts of Islam out to light.

-Well listen, you have to be very careful then. Are you sure that the bounty on your head is real.

-I am sure. My mother got word to me through Yaseen my cousin. You know Yaseen doesn't care about these things one way or another. He is really an agnostic. He has seen enough of extreme Islam to stay away from it. He just doesn't dare reveal his true feelings.

-Ah Yaseen, good, good.. He is a decent man. I like him.

-Well, let's stop this talk now and get ready. I will stop by your house in two hours to pick you up.

-Ok then. See you.

Chapter 4

Hazem and Daoud entered the main door of the hospital and went to the reception desk and asked for Fadi's room. They were directed to the room and given temporary passes. They silently went up the elevator to the third floor. No words were exchanged. They were like schoolboys caught in a bad act and were being led to the principal's office.

They came off the elevator and turned a right corner just past the nurse's station. They approached room 3014 where Fadi is and saw that the door was slightly ajar. They heard a deep voice singing quietly: Great is your faithfulness Oh Lord my father, morning by morning new mercies I see…

They looked at each other and immediately tears started to come to their eyes. Cancer had not broken his spirit, nor did it diminish his faith. He is still singing one of his favorite hymns.

They pushed on through the door, and as he heard them enter the room, he opened his eyes. A slow, very wide smile came to his face. His eyes twinkled with a spark and a sly, mischievous look came upon his face:

-So, there you are you two useless friends. I have been here for 5 days, and you just showed up. Where were you?

Hazem said: We weren't sure you would be happy to see us while in bed. We know how tough you are and that you don't like to be fussed over.

Daoud broke into the conversation with a laugh and said: If we knew you would look this sexy, we would have come in long before now.

-Oh, shut up you goof off. Fadi threw the cap of a juice bottle at Daoud. "You are just a coward. You couldn't face the fact that your friend may be dying."

Hazem commented: You never stop kidding around do you Fadi? You are just looking for attention. Few more days and you will be back like before. Stronger than a horse.

Fadi said: See what I mean. You guys are cowards. Why don't you face the truth like I have? And since when do we fear death. We treaded in its shadows for years. It knocked on our doors many times before. We should have been afraid back then when we had no idea what would happen to us afterwards, but now that we know where we are going. Death to me is gain.

Daoud said: We know, but we still like to have you in our lives for a while longer. Don't give up just yet. Hold on man. You will get through this.

-Whether I get through this or not doesn't matter. What matters to me is Lila. I don't need to tell you guys to look after her. She is your sister now and I want you to help her. I know that she will grieve for me. I don't want her to do that. I will be with my savior in Heaven. That is where I want to be now. No need to cry. Sooner or later, I will see all of you there.

Daoud said: let's hope later rather than sooner. I have a few things to do yet. The three laughed heartily.

Hazem and Daoud said goodbye to Fadi. He felt good now. His friends' visit brought back good memories to him. It seems now that he had known both of them forever. They were his closest friends now, but there was a day when they were all enemies fighting on opposite sides.

His thoughts trailed back to Lebanon again. To a time in his life when he was a different man fighting a different battle.

Chapter 5

It was 1976 in Lebanon and the heavy artillery rounds could be heard in the southern sector of the Beqaa Valley. Round after round lighted the night sky and spurts of gun fire broke the silence and interrupted the sounds of crickets. The cool air of the valley was mixed with the scent of wildflowers and gun powder. A coyote dashed through the sage brushes just as two armed men wove back and forth through the heavy vegetation. They wore combat dress and covered their heads with Selougs (Bedouin head dress). They had guns holstered to their wastes and gun belts strapped around their upper body. They both held Kalashnikov's that looked much used and worn. The barrels were, however, clean and shiny and the mechanisms well-oiled and cared for. These were fighting men accustomed to weapons and their use. They were also very familiar with this land and did not seem to be disturbed by the sounds around them, nor the smell of gun powder and death in the air. They were moving north towards the highway. They heard reports of Christian Kataeb militia moving about in the area and wanted some blood. Fahd was a Palestinian refugee who had lived all his life in Lebanon. He was born and raised in the refugee camps. He knew nothing but hunger, frustration and anger throughout his life. He heard the old people talk of the old country. How they were driven out of their lands and farms. Their homes and orange groves. Their lands taken by force by Jews coming mostly from Europe and America and some from Russia. They were heavily armed and helped by the British. They came in and butchered the land and took what they wanted from it. Some of the Palestinian occupants fought and died, others fled. They had no place to go to. Just like the Jews once were without a country they could call home, now they too had their own Diaspora.

Fadi his companion was Lebanese to the bone. His parents and grandparents and many generations before them were born in Lebanon. He was fighting this war for a different reason. It seems that he and Fahd shared the same enemies, however.

Fadi whispered to his companion, Fahd; I can hear sounds in the near distance, not more than 100 meters away.

Fahd replied: That is strange. I did not think we would run into those dogs so soon. I thought they were at least one or two kilometers ahead.

-Well, I am sure of what I heard. Be careful, let's not make any noise. Approach slowly and keep behind the brush.

Fahd growled: I would like to get my hand on one or two of them, tie them up then have fun cutting them into small pieces.

-We are not animals. I had Christian friends once and they were not that bad. It is this damned war that turned everyone into an insane blood thirsty demon.

Fahd growled once more and shoved Fadi hard. Damn you! Why do you defend those dogs? I swear if I hear you mention your Christian friends one more time, I will put this Kalashnikov in your belly and fire a full cartridge.

Fadi looked at him sadly and said: don't you remember how my Christian friends used to come to your camp and bring food and blankets and desserts with them. Have you forgotten how the nuns rescued us from that gang of Kataeb dogs and hid us in their monastery for eight days? They fed us and took care of us even though they knew we were Moslems. Not one hard word was uttered to us. Even when they send us off, they gave us bread and olives and sent us in peace.

Fahd looked on thoughtfully for a minute then sighed and said: You are right about those nuns. Even with my heart so full of hate and anger, I couldn't but feel respect for them. They were so full of love and kindness despite all this hell around us. When they spoke to me about God and his love and how we should love and respect other people and other religions, I could see the sincerity in their eyes. I felt so ashamed every time they spoke to me. They were so humble, clean and righteous. Oh, why did you mention them to me? Now I will lose some of my fire.

Fadi shushed him again. They were very close now. He could even smell a mixture of sweat and cigarette smoke nearby. They got down on their bellies and started crawling over the wet grass. They could clearly hear the sounds of cursing and laughter now. They could even see the glow of cigarettes not more than ten meters from where they were. They counted five well-armed men.

They came behind the five men then slowly stood to their knees and opened with a burst of fire. The five men were caught by surprise. As they turned backwards to fire, bullets hit their bodies and smashed their skulls. Within seconds, the attack was over, and all five men were on the ground. Fahd jumped quickly to the fallen men and checked them for signs of life. The first three were face down in the ground and dead. The fourth one was on his back with his eyes open and glaring at the sky. There was no movement and no breathing. Fahd spat in his eyes then slashed his face with his knife. Fadi was beside the fifth man. There were no signs of life in this man also. He turned around to tell Fahd that this man was also dead, and he was struck by an ugly and cruel site. Fahd looked like a hungry animal feasting on a fresh kill. He was slashing and stabbing into the bodies of the dead men with a twisted grin. He did not appear human at all. Blood had covered his hands and parts of his face. Fadi shuddered at the site. He looked down at the fallen man beside him and felt guilt and remorse. Why did he kill him? What had this man ever done to him? He yelled at Fahd to stop, and Fahd just looked straight at him as if he was looking at emptiness, then sat down and looked at his bloody hands, then looked again at Fadi, then easily rolled down to his right side and closed his eyes and in very few minutes he was soundly sleeping next to the dead men. Fadi was bewildered by the site. This does not make any sense. This whole war is insane. Fahd was insane. But then what was he? Did he not also fire at these men and participate in killing them. Had he so far not killed more than fifty men? Men with families. Men with wives and children maybe? Men with mothers and fathers who will weep after them. What has happened to him? Had he not recently been to Beirut and seen Lila there. Lila his angel. Lila his salvation from all this hatred and war. Is Lila not a Christian? What would she do if she saw him now, hands bloodied and sinful? Would she still love him? Would she still call him Habibi? Would she still look at him with her pure hazel eyes and childish smile, or would she shun him and loathe him? He could not dare to think about that. He will never let her see this side of himself. With that determination, he took about twenty steps away from the dead and laid down himself. He put his arm under his head and exhausted, he went to sleep dreaming of a world far different from his present one and dreaming of a time past.

Chapter·6

Fadi woke up early morning with a terrible hunger. He felt as if he hadn't eaten for days. He got up, shook his head and looked around. He saw the bodies of the five men they killed the night before and his friend sleeping next to one of them. He looked so comfortable and peaceful as if he was sleeping in his own bed without a care in the world.

Fahd had become a blood thirsty killer. He was no longer a human being. He had an appetite for murder that Fadi had not seen before. It seems that his friend now will go out of his way to find people to kill. He started targeting Druz, Christians of all sects even if they were not Kataeb, and even Moslems who were calling for an end to the war.

There were people on all sides who wanted peace and wanted to stop this senseless war. They were saying that all Lebanese are brothers and that if they had differences, they should resolve them with reason and dialogue. It seems however that these voices were drowned out swiftly by the louder voices and bullets of those with much hatred and vengeance in their hearts.

But where was he from all this? Was he not a blood-thirsty killer himself? How many men has he killed in battle so far, and how many in cold blood? He still can't forgive himself for shooting Saleem!

Saleem was from his village. Fadi came upon him as he was trying to fix his motorcycle. He was situated behind his house at the edge of the village beneath an olive tree. He had parts of the cycle on the ground and was busy trying to undo a stubborn nut on the motor housing. He saw Fadi approaching. He had his gun on a seat close to him but did not attempt to reach it. He thought that he was safe with Fadi, after all, Fadi was from his village, and they were friends at one time. They went to the same school, ditched classes together to go hunting for birds with their sling shots. They swam in the river together and at times shared punishment for mischief that they both did together. Since the war started however, they became on opposite sides. Saleem told Fadi one time that Lebanon is a Christian country and that no Palestinian will take one centimeter of Lebanese soil without bloodshed to the knees.

Fadi hated Palestinians as much as Saleem did, but he did not like Lebanon being called a Christian country. Lebanon was an Arab country and belonged to the Moslems. Even if the history of Lebanon was clearly different. This may have been alright with Fadi before the war started, but now that he is fighting a Jihad (holy war) he can't let friendship come between him and his performance of his duties as a Moslem.

He pointed his gun at Saleem and said: Saleem, for the sake of the old days, I am going to give you a chance. Repent and turn to the only true religion and become my brother in Islam. We will then fight Jihad on the same side and give our lives for Allah instead of fighting on opposite sides.

Saleem answered: Are you insane Fadi. I was born a Christian and will die as a Christian. You have known me throughout your life to be a Christian and we were friends. What has changed now that you come at me with a gun? Our fight is not with each other, it is with the Palestinians to whom we gave refuge and are now trying to take over our country.

Fadi looked at him for a moment with some hesitation, then remembered the words of his Imam "Christians and Jews are the enemies of Allah and Allah will only be pleased by their total annihilation. It is the duty of every good Moslem to fight the holy war and bring Lebanon to Islam. We can't leave Lebanon in the hands of Kufar (Infidels). It is the only Arabic country not ruled by Islam and it is a thorn in the side of the Umma (combined nation) of Islam.

Fadi lifted his Kalashnikov slowly and aimed it at Saleem with cold and empty eyes. His heart was without emotion. He looked at Saleem as if he was looking at a void and aimed at his chest. He then saw a faint disbelieving smile come over Saleem's face as if he thought that his former friend was joking. The smile then slowly vanished as Saleem looked into the eyes of Fadi and saw murder in them. His eyes became filled with fear as Fadi continued to aim, then fired. Bewilderment and disbelief covered Saleem's face as he looked at Fadi then down at his bloodied shirt as he touched the blood to see if it was real or if he was dreaming. He looked back at his friend Fadi with a faint smile, then tumbled backwards and died.

Fadi was now remembering his friend's eyes. How could he have gotten to this point? How could he have become so hateful and vengeful?

He started to remind himself that he was doing this for Allah and that it was his duty. Allah is pleased with him for striking the enemies of Islam.

As he told himself that, he felt a small measure of relief, although a voice deep within him was telling him that he is wrong.

Fahd started to wake up. He looked at the dead man besides him and kicked him saying out loud: one less Christian dog to worry about and laughed. Fadi grinned back at him then pulled his Kalashnikov to his shoulder as his companion got ready, then they moved on.

They walked briskly then trotted. The slope before them was easy. They could smell the wildflowers and grass in the cold morning air. This was a beautiful country. Beautiful in every respect. The mountainous terrain studded with majestic cedar trees some over a thousand years old, proclaiming the uniqueness of this land. Plum and almond trees spread branches that were covered with white flowers while olive and lemon trees and ever-flowing shrubs added to this exotic mixture of greenery. As you go down into the valley, wild oregano and sage covered the descending slopes amidst an explosion of wildflowers of all colors and patches of Lavender stalks swaying in the breeze and dancing better than any belly dancer the world had to offer. Fragrance filling the atmosphere. Flowing streams of ice-cold water looked like shiny ribbons that were tossed in a random fashion over the landscape.

On the western slopes grass ran downward to the sparkling jade sea as a lover running to meet her long lost love and take him into her arms. Villages covered the slopes with their crimson red roofs and whitewashed walls surrounded with orange and lemon trees and grape vines. Sounds of singing, laughter and music used to fill this now prevailing silence that is only shattered periodically by the sounds of Katousha rockets and gunfire.

They came upon a small house whose outside walls were riddled with bullets and a portion of an upper room had been blown out most likely by a rocket or RPJ (rocket propelled grenade). The smell of fresh baked bread and something cooking on an open fire had filled the air. They were hungry before they came upon the house but now, they were vanquished. Their stomachs started to growl, and their mouths became wet with saliva. As they carefully approached the house, a small, statured, old lady came out of the door-way slowly limping on her right side. She was wearing an all-black dress with a light brown woolen jacket thrown over her shoulders. Most of her teeth were missing and her wrinkled face, neck and hands showed her age to be quite advanced. A small cross was tattooed on her forehead. She heard them approach and looked towards the two men straining her old sparkly eyes for better vision:

"Who, Who's there. From where are you? Are you hungry? Come here grandchildren, I just made some Shourbat Adas (lentil soup). Come inside and eat. You must be very hungry. How far did you travel?

They looked at each other then lowered their weapons and followed her inside. They were immediately greeted by a very clean and organized room with a wooden table, a sofa and several chairs. There was also a bed and a large wooden box next to the bed. There was a wooden cross on the wall and several pictures of the Virgin Mary with child and images of different saints.

As they sat down at the table, she placed three loaves of fresh baked bread before them then placed a pot filled with steaming soup and two empty round bowls. They did not wait for any silver wear. They immediately took the bread and started dipping pieces of it in the pot and eating. She looked at them fondly and laughed showing her missing teeth. "I am glad you like my soup. Don't burn your tongues, it is steaming hot."

They did not even answer her. They kept on eating. She brought them a large dry onion which Fadi split in half by smacking it down with his closed fist. No words or glances were exchanged. It was serious business now. This was some of the best food they had tasted in a very, very long time.

They finished eating and asked the lady if they could take a nap somewhere. She looked thoughtfully at both, then told them to follow her. She took them to what appeared to be her son's room. There were two small beds in there and a table between the two beds, and on the table, there was a framed picture of a handsome, dark haired young man with a black ribbon on the corner of the picture frame and an open Bible, and the page read:

"You have heard that it was said, 'Love your neighbor and hate your enemy.' But I tell you, love your enemies and pray for those who persecute you, that you may be children of your Father in heaven. He causes his sun to rise on the evil and the good and sends rain on the righteous and the unrighteous. ...

Chapter 7

Fadi and Fahd slept for what seemed to be an eternity. They woke up late into the night. There was a fresh breeze coming into the room from the partially opened window. They went outside and washed their faces with water from the well. The old lady came out and asked them if they wanted tea. They nodded and she went back inside. They started discussing what their next step should be. Fahd said that they should take whatever food she has in the house and leave quickly. He said that since she was hospitable to them, they should not kill her.

Fadi was displeased with what he had heard. He did not want to hurt the old lady in any way. He wanted to leave her in peace. She reminded him much of his own grandmother. She was very tender, loving and generous and he was unwilling to treat her in such a way.

Fahd said that if they take her food, it would be "Halal" since she is a Christian.

Fadi said to Fahd: How dare you even think in such a way. Don't you know that Allah is watching? How could he be pleased with us treating her in this way after she fed us and welcomed us? You should be ashamed of your thoughts.

Fahd replied: It does not matter how she treated us. She is still our enemy and she should die.

Fadi answered: She is no body's enemy. She is a lonely widow that is full of love and generosity. Leave her alone. Let's leave right now and forget about the tea or using any more of her resources. We can find food somewhere else.

-We are not going anywhere. We need to finish this together. Let her prepare us dinner first, then we take what we need and tie her up and leave.

-We will not touch a hair on her head.

Fadi lifted his Kalashnikov and stared at Fahd. An ugly look came over Fahd's face as he looked at the Kalashnikov and then at Fadi's eyes. There was no wavering in his eyes and Fahd knew that his companion was dead serious. He also knew that they were in hostile territory and that he needed him.

-Alright. Let's not fight over this. Let's go have our tea and then we will leave peacefully.

Inside the house the old lady had prepared some olives and Za'tar for them to eat with the tea. She asked them to sit down at the table, then she placed several loaves of flat bread on the table and sat down herself to a cup of tea. They ate their full while drinking tea. The olives and Za'tar were fresh and made by the old lady herself from her own olive tree and from wild herbs from the mountain side. It tasted amazing for such a simple dish.

-Where are you going from here grandchildren? The old woman asked.

Fadi answered: We will be going to the east, as he looked down at his cup of tea. He did not want to tell her what he really wanted to do, which was to go further north and hunt some more Kataeb soldiers.

She looked him straight in the eyes and said to him: Those who live by the sword, shall perish by the sword. Living for the sake of killing and revenge is worse than death itself, grandson.

Those words pierced his heart and soul. His eyes winced in pain. He remembered his sister. The old woman talked to him as if she knew. But how could she have known.

He told her that revenge at times is the best course for justice. And he wanted justice. His thirst for blood was not born out of nothing.

He had a sister once. Her name was Dalia. She was 10 years younger than he was and she was his pride and joy. His parents had only one other child between them who was only two years younger than Fadi and died of Diphtheria. His parents stopped having children for a while, then Dalia was born. She brought new life to the household. She brightened every day of their lives with her smile, never-ending energy and the love she received from them, and she gave in return.

She was only 16 years old when it happened. It was at the beginning of the war. She was going to see her cousin Souad in Zahle. She went there with her aunt Zahra. They took a Taxicab with two other people from a nearby village. On the way to Zahle they were stopped by a group of Kataeb militia. One of the militia men had just lost his brother in Southern Beirut when he was killed by a Moslem neighbor. He was walking down the street when a Moslem neighbor who had a small argument with him that morning went down the street behind him and struck him just below the back of his neck with a meat cleaver. He did not die instantly. He fell to the ground and was shaking violently for almost 10 minutes before he died. When his Kataeb brother came to get him, he swore that he would not let his body get cold before he took revenge. He was true to his word. The man that killed his brother did not live through the hour. He went to his home and threw in two hand grenades that killed his brother's murderer and his wife as well. But that did not satisfy his need for revenge.

When the Taxi cab was stopped at the barricade, he checked the ID cards. Dalia and her aunt refused to give their IDs and told the Kataeb soldiers to be damned. They were immediately taken about

20 meters away behind a clump of trees and guns placed to their heads. They were both shot once in the forehead and immediately died. Their bodies were found almost a full week later by a villager. Their IDs were still on them.

When Fadi went to get their bodies, he took his cousin Hamed with him. He would never forget that accursed day. It was the day he turned into a different man. Fadi who was quite, funny and gentle became a monster filled with hatred and violence and anger. The sight of his dead sister and aunt changed him forever. These were hard memories.

The words of the old woman now echoed in his mind again. He knew that this cycle of revenge would not end. The more blood he shed, the thirstier for blood and revenge he became.

She looked at him again and said that forgiveness and love are much better than hatred and revenge. She said: Anyone can hate. Anyone is capable of killing. We can justify killing for the sake of revenge or the sake of religion, but God is the God of love and forgiveness. His way is better. If we can only experience and realize how much God loves us then we can pass that same kind of love to others. There would be no more killing, and no more need for revenge. She told Fadi and Fahd: I know that you are not Christians. All those people who call themselves Christians and hate and kill others are also not Christians. Christ said that those who love him will obey his commandments, and his most important commandment is to love and forgive others.

Fadi looked at her with tearful eyes. He was sick of killing. His hatred for Christians had only grown over the last few years. All the killing he had done did not make his hatred any less. But his soul was in anguish, and he was in pain. He was tired of the bloodshed. This old woman's words were new to him. How could he even think about love and forgiveness after what happened to his sister and aunt? Yet how many fathers and mothers and sisters and brothers had he deprived of loved ones?

He remembered the words he read in the open Bible, and they seemed to burn deep in his memory and in his heart "You have heard that it was said, 'Love your neighbor and hate your enemy.' But I tell you, love your enemies and pray for those who persecute you, that you may be children of your Father in heaven. He causes his sun to rise on the evil and the good and sends rain on the righteous and the unrighteous".

As he was pondering on these words, Hazem walked into the room.

Chapter 8

Hazem was tall and slender. He had a dark face. He had a scar on the right cheek. His eyebrows were thick, his eyes piercing. He had a long and curved nose with a thick and hairy mustache that was curved upwards on both ends. He had no beard but was not clean shaven. He wore jeans and a leather jacket and was very energetic. He had no weapons. He came into the room with a wide smile on his face. He came immediately to the old woman and hugged her tightly and kissed her on the cheeks then kissed her hands. She kissed his forehead and patted him on the shoulder. Her wrinkled face had come alive when she saw him as if he was a long-lost son that had finally come home.

He looked to his right side then and saw Fadi and Fahd. His smile continued and did not diminish.

-God Bless You. I am Hazem, who are you?

Fadi and Fahd wearily introduced themselves. They looked at each other then frowned. He did not display any weapons, but they did not know if he had a gun or a hidden weapon below that jacket. Fahd's gun slowly rose to waist level under the table. Fahd asked Hazem if he was the old woman's son.

Hazem answered: I am her son, but not by physical birth. She did not give birth to my body, but to my soul. He laughed out loud.

Fadi frowned and asked: What do you mean?

-I mean that the only blood relationship between me and her is the blood of Christ. She is not a relation of mine. She is the person who found me in the woods when I was shot and dying and brought me back here and nursed me back to life. But more importantly, she showed me how to seek and find eternal life.

Fadi and Fahd looked at each other again. These were strange words, and they did not like hearing them. Furthermore, they did not know how to treat this newcomer. They did not want to cause the old woman any harm, but they did not like what this man was saying, and they wanted to kill him.

Hazem continued: I was separated from my friends when we engaged a group of other fighters. We did not know who they were. We thought that they were Druz or Syrian. They started firing at us before we could talk. I saw two of my friends fall immediately, then I was hit hard in my right shoulder and spun around and fell on my face. It was two days later that Umm George found me and took me to her house.

This was the first time that they heard her name. Fadi wondered if it was her son George's picture that was next to the bible on the table.

Hazem continued: imagine my surprise when I woke up in her son's room and on his bed with my wounds cleaned and bandaged. I had a fever and was delirious for several days, but I could remember seeing her by my side and hearing her talk to me. I remembered her feeding me soup and cleaning my wounds daily. She had told me that the bullet that hit me went out of the other side of my shoulder. It was the infection that followed that kept me in bed for almost three weeks.

Fadi then asked him carefully with a menacing look in his eyes: then you are a Kataeb militiaman. Fahd's grip tightened over his Kalashnikov and his finger started to slowly tighten over the trigger.

To their amazement, Hazem said that he was not a Kataeb militiaman, but a Moslem fighter from Syria that came over to Lebanon to help his Moslem brothers fight the holy war. He had crossed over from

Msherfi and into Lebanon and immediately joined a group of fighters from the Beqaa Valley. They had made many raids on remote villages and on some military targets. He was injured in one of these raids.

Fadi was bewildered by this revelation. How could this young Moslem fighter be here and be received with such warmth and love by this Christian woman. Did she not know his story?

Fadi asked Umm George: Didn't you know that he was a Moslem fighter killing Christian soldiers? Why did you not surrender him to the militias when you found him, and why did you receive us in such a hospitable way. I know that you were not afraid of us even though you should have been. What is your secret? You speak of love in the midst of hate and violence. You give kindness and mercy in the middle of war and destruction. You rejoice despite all this terrible darkness that surrounds all of us. This doesn't make any sense.

Umm George smiled mildly and looked at Fadi with old eyes that shone with love and life and said:

-This wasn't always the case. There was a time when I too could have surrendered to hate. My son George was a bank employee in Beirut. He was as gentle as a dove. He was full of goodness. He spent his entire life trying to help people. He never cared whether the person he was helping is Lebanese or Palestinian, Christian, Moslem or Jewish. Always extended himself to others. He was so humble. He would drink tea often with the maintenance man at the bank and would give the poor odd jobs so that they could make some money. Everybody who knew him loved him. One day he was coming out of the bank and a sniper killed him with one bullet between the eyes. When he was brought back to me like that, a part of me also died. Such a precious life lost for no reason at all except that he was a Christian and a Moslem sniper wanted to kill some Christians.

I almost cursed all Moslems that day. Then I was so ashamed of my reaction. How could I blame all Moslems for a murder that was committed by just one? I also remembered how many innocent

Moslems were killed by vengeful Christians and then how many Druz and Syrians. How many Jews were also being killed and killing Palestinians and Arabs? I saw all this turmoil and hatred and I asked myself: Why are they killing each other. Why are Christians, Jews and Moslems filled with such animosity towards each other? Aren't they all Children of Abraham?

I could not bring myself to hate anyone. Jesus had taught me how to love. This is why I always keep the bible open next to my son's picture. It is always open to the same verse. To remind me of who I am. I am a child of God. A follower of Jesus Christ who had given his own life as a sacrifice of love to bring us closer to God and closer to each other.

Fahd stood angrily when he heard of the sacrifice of Jesus. He as a Moslem did not believe that Jesus died on the cross. He believed that Jesus (Issa Ibn Meriam) was a favored profit of God and that when the Jews tried to crucify him, Allah made a switch and it was Judas Iscariot who was crucified instead, while Jesus was lifted alive to heaven. He called Umm George an infidel. He raised his weapon and attempted to fire. Fadi was quicker, however. He threw himself against Fahd and slapped the weapon out of his hand, while Hazem quickly jumped in and twisted Fahd's hand behind his back and held him in a choke hold. After disarming him, Fadi took his other gun and two hand grenades from him and told him to leave. He no longer wanted to be with him. He was a murderer who cared not whom he killed. He was blood thirsty and enraged. Fadi told him that if he ever saw him again, he would kill him.

Fahd went into a rage and started cursing and spitting at all of them, promising to come back and do the worst things possible to all of them. Umm George, tears streaming down her cheeks told him: May God forgive you grandson. I will pray for your soul and for you not to kill anymore and not to be killed yourself. You need to forgive in order to be yourself forgiven.

He stumbled out of the door still cursing. Hazem looked after him and shook his head. Fadi was still reeking with anger. This woman had every right to hate them. Yet here she was treating them as if they were her own children. She actually let them sleep in her son's room and in his bed. How could he hate such a person? And how could such a person be an infidel?

He looked at her and said: forgive us grandmother. You were so kind to us. I beg your forgiveness.

She took his face into her hands and kissed him on top of his head and whispered "I Love you"

He started weeping. He had not heard these words said to him for years. His life has been so devoid of love and emotions. His soul was dry and thirsty. These simple words were like a rush of cold water that suddenly swept over a barren and dry land. He soaked the words in. He looked at her and hugged her and let go of his emotions. He cried and cried till no more tears came out...

Chapter 9

Hazem watched Fahd go down the trail still swearing and cursing as he turned his head back once in a while. Hazem watched him until he finally disappeared at a fork in the road where the main road to Rose's house forked off into the fields. He went back inside the house then. Fadi had finally taken hold of his emotions. He was sitting on a chair and Rose (Umm George) was sitting beside him talking to him. When he saw Hazem, he immediately asked him: Have you changed your religion.

Hazem said: If you mean by that have, I become a follower of Christ, then yes. It is not about religion. It is about the salvation of your soul. I was always a religious person before. I thought only about doing my duties as a Moslem hoping that when I die God might be merciful enough to spare me from hell. Deep inside however I always thought that I would wind up there. Look, if our Prophet himself and his companions were not sure whether they would go to heaven or not, then how could I have been sure. I didn't want to leave my eternity to chance, I wanted to be sure.

Fadi said: And are you sure now?

-Yes, I am. I have no doubt whatsoever now. It makes complete sense to me. God created us and he loves us. He wants us to be eternal beings and to be with him. That makes sense to me. If I painted a picture and it was a good picture, I would want to keep it with me. If it was a bad picture, I may paint over it or toss it away. But that is me. A wretched, full of faults human being. God on the other hand created mankind as a superior being. He breathed life into him from his own nostrils. Creation is amazing and mankind is the most amazing creation of all.

-But what about all the evil that we do. I often think that I deserve hell, even though I don't want to go there. How could I even dream of forgiveness from God after all I have done?

-We may not deserve forgiveness, but God offers it to us anyway. He is a Just God who hates sin and deplores unrighteousness. But he also loves us without any bounds. I believe that he took the only step possible in order to grant us forgiveness while keeping with his righteousness. He offered his son Jesus as a sacrifice sufficient for the forgiveness of sins of all mankind, if you are willing to accept his forgiveness.

-Who wouldn't accept God's forgiveness when it is so freely offered?

Hazem looked at Fadi thoughtful and said: The people that reject God the most are those who are the most religious.

Fadi was shocked at that comment. How could the religious people who spend their entire lives trying to please God be the ones who reject him the most?

Hazem continued: Those who sin a lot know that they have no hope whatsoever in redeeming themselves. They often look for mercy knowing fully well that all they deserve is brute justice from God. When they hear of the good news of God's salvation, they are overwhelmed by his love and forgiveness. Jesus said: "He that is forgiven much, loves much". The religious people on the other hand often think that they know everything and that they are so righteous that they don't need mercy. That is the most dangerous lie of all. If man can please God by his own righteousness, then such a God can't be much more righteous than man. We fall very short of the measure of holiness and righteousness set by God. That is why we need a savior and a redeemer. That is why God in the fullness of his majesty came into our world through a virgin without the carnal will of mankind. He lived among humans as one of them. Ate as they do and breathed as they do. Suffered thirst and hunger and lack of sleep. He worked and made a living for himself. All in order to experience all the trials of human beings and live without sin, thus qualifying himself as a substitute for mankind. He lived a life without sin and became therefore a perfect sacrifice. A sinless offering in our stead, that all our sins and inequities can be placed upon him. When he died on the cross, my sins were placed upon him. He paid the price of my sins for me. His blood was atonement for my sins. If I accept that and turn from my ways, surrender my life and heart to his love, I will be saved and when the day comes and I leave this life, I have no doubt that I will spend eternity in his presence.

Fadi became somewhat irritated and said: That is blasphemy Hazem. How could God be born from a woman, and how could he die. If he died, then he was not God.

Hazem said: You must understand the nature of God Fadi. He is not bound like us by time and space. He came to this world through Jesus who was born from the Virgin Mary. Moslems call him Issa Ibn Meriam. According to the Quran, Isa is the Word of God and a spirit from him. It is not much different from what Christians believe. The Gospel of John says, "In the beginning was the Word, and the Word was with God, and the Word was God". God the father, Jesus the son and the Holy Spirit are one. They are God. You cannot separate one from another. The best way I could explain this to you Fadi is by using the example of the sun. It has body or mass; it has light and it has warmth. You can look at each of these three things separately. You can see the light of the sun without feeling its warmth if you were inside a cooled house. Or if you close your eyes, you may feel its warmth without seeing its light. When you look at the sun, you see its body, its round shape. All these three together are the sun. The three characters of the sun may be referred to separately, but one can't be present without the other.

Fadi said: But if Jesus was the son of God, and you can't separate God from himself, then what happened when Jesus died? Where did God go? Was he then divided? I am confused.

Hazem laughed: Look at it this way Fadi. When you enjoy the sunlight and soak in its warmth, does that diminish the sun? When the light shines into our world day after day, does that make the sun less than what it actually is?

-No, it doesn't. Then, are you telling me that when Jesus died on the cross it was only his carnal body that died, but he remained alive.

-It is always the body that dies Fadi, but we never die. Our spirits and souls live forever. This is why you are so special to God. He created you to live forever. Death was not God's design for mankind. Death is the result of sin. We were created to be in the likeness of God. That means we were created to be eternal and moral beings.

Fadi was yearning to learn more. He had thought about God, about life and death, about the meaning of existence a thousand times. He was never able to reach a conclusion. He always felt lost and confused whenever these questions arose. Now he is hearing for the first time about the nature of God, the Love of God, and the sacrifice of God. He had never thought about God in these terms before. God to him was always a distant master who looked down from heaven angrily and wrathfully at all mankind. He feared God and thought of him as a tyrant who was ready to smite him whenever he sinned. Now he felt as if a veil was being lifted slowly from before his eyes, and he was seeing the sunlight for the first time.

Hazem continued: You can block the sun light by using some object. That doesn't mean that you killed the sun light. That only means that you hid it from your own existence. This was the way when Jesus died. He was absent from our existence, but he did not cease to exist.

God the father, Jesus the son and the Holy Spirit are not three but one. We Christians believe in One God. We don't believe in three gods like some Moslems think.

Fadi said: I always thought of it as blasphemy when Christians used the words "son of God" God does not have children!

Hazem smiled gently and said: God has many children. You can be one of them if you choose to. When we say that Jesus is the son of God, or that we are the children of God, this has nothing to do with reproduction. It is a word used only in a spiritual sense to describe that Jesus was not born from man and woman but from the spirit of God descending upon the Virgin Mary. It is very offensive to Christians when Moslems think that Christians believe that God had a carnal relationship with Mary and Jesus was born that way. This is not a Christian concept and is considered utter blasphemy by all Christians. We are God's children through his grace and mercy. Through faith and confession that God appeared in the flesh through Jesus Christ, and that Jesus offered himself as a sacrifice for our sins, that he was crucified and that he rose from death on the third day because he was without sin. If you accept that Fadi, you too can become a child of God.

Fadi was absorbing all that was being said. His heart was beating very fast. Could this be what he was searching for all his life? He wanted to believe. The bible verse he read opened his eyes to something he had never experienced before. The words told him to love his enemies and pray for them. He had not known anything but hatred before that. Nothing but a thirst for revenge, yet that thirst was never satisfied. He believed in God, but his fear of him made him feel abandoned and rejected by God. For the first time in his life he is hearing that God is a loving father rather than a vengeful master.

Hazem continued: Jesus said, "Come to me all ye that labor and are heavily laden and I will give you rest" He also said: "I am the bread of life. Whoever comes to me will never go hungry, and whoever believes in me will never be thirsty.

Fadi broke down. He was heavily burdened, hungry and thirsty. The words of Jesus touched his soul. He wanted to be free of hate and sin. Wanted his thirst and hunger for peace and forgiveness to be satisfied. He had hated Christians before, but he found himself suddenly unable to hate anymore. He knelt by Hazem and lifted his head up to heaven and shouted with all his might: God have mercy on me I am a sinner. Jesus give me from your water so I may never thirst again. Take my sins away. Save me.

He started sobbing as Hazem and Umm George took him into their arms. Then came the sounds of gun fire….

Chapter · 10

Fahd went around the corner at the end of the descending pathway towards the fields. He was so filled with anger and hate that he could barely stay sane. He wanted to kill all of them and especially that dog Fadi. That infidel lover. How could he side with Christians against his Moslem brother? He deserves to die. Fahd wanted to kill him, and he wanted to kill him now. He could not take a chance to lose him.

He had no weapons now except for his boot knife. It was a good, razor-sharp knife by which he could do plenty of damage. But Fadi was a tough fighter, and he had a Kalashnikov with him. He had to get a gun if he was to be able to kill Fadi.

He continued to weave his way through the fields. Most of the fields had stone boundaries separating them. Walls of blue-gray stones that were knee to waste high. Once in while he would see some movement among the stones. A small lizard or snake. On top of one of these walls he saw the freshly shed skin of a large snake. The skin had a unique black and golden pattern on it. He was careful now. The last thing he wanted was to be bit by a snake.

Suddenly he heard a sound nearby. It was the sound of cloth rubbing against grass. He knelt quickly behind one of the walls. Slowly, an old man approached. He was walking slowly and humming a melody. He had a shot gun strapped to his shoulder for protection. Fahd thought that this was a great opportunity for him to get a weapon. It was not a Kalashnikov, but it had fire power.

He approached the old man and said: Salam Alaikum

The old man looked him up and down, then returned his greeting and asked: From where are you?

Fahd did not have time to enter into a conversation. His blood was boiling, and he wanted revenge. He struck the old man very hard with his fist and knocked him unconscious. He took the shot gun away from him and checked it. It was loaded with two cartridges. He checked the old man's pockets for more cartridges and found three more. He pocketed them, took the old man's loose tobacco and the makings for cigarettes and some matches. There was no money on the old man.

He left him lying in the field and returned towards Umm George's house. He was now trotting. He had an animal like instinct when it came to killing. He did not hesitate, and he had no remorse. He had lost his humanity long ago. Killing to him was now as normal as eating, drinking and sleeping.

He approached the gate, and it was still open. He walked into the yard quickly and then ran to the eastern wall of the house and knelt down listening for sounds. He heard Fadi praying. He was shocked. This was no Moslem prayer. As a matter of fact, it was a prayer unlike he had ever heard before. He stopped dead in his tracks. He was confused. He never heard Fadi pray so earnestly before. He stood up slowly and took the shot gun into his hands. He slowly cocked the two barrels and came quickly into the door. He smiled as he pointed his gun to Fadi's chest and began to squeeze the trigger. Hazem was quicker as he immediately grabbed a small wooden chair and flung it into Fahd's face. Fahd moved quickly to avoid the chair and in doing so he discharged his weapon.

Umm George had seen the gun come up slowly before Hazem grabbed the chair, and she moved swiftly into the line of fire to protect Fadi. As the shot gun discharged, she was sprayed with pellets and blood immediately gushed from her neck and chest and trickled down to the floor from underneath the arms of her garment. Fadi grabbed her as she was falling and held her in his arms and let out a horrifying scream. This good woman that brought him back to life and brought peace and forgiveness to his soul can't die now, and like this!!

Fahd was now reaching into his right-side pocket for two more shells. Hazem did not give him a chance. He lunged at him and took him to the floor. The two struggled but Hazem was stronger and was also furious. He struck Fahd below his rib cage several times with his big strong fists. Fahd could no longer breathe and pulled his knees to his chest to protect himself. Hazem quickly got up and picked up Fadi's Kalashnikov and fired several shots into the dirt near Fahd's face. Dirt kicked up and stung Fahd in the face. Fahd quivered with fear and anger. He wanted to get up again and fight but found no strength within himself to do so. He slowly sat up and leaned onto the door jamb and looked up at Hazem, then looked sideways towards Umm George and Fadi.

Life had already left Umm George and Fadi was holding her close to his chest and crying. His tears were falling on her face and mixing with her blood. Despite the damage to her face, she looked peaceful, and she seemed to be smiling. She had succeeded not only in saving his soul, but also his life.

After a few minutes he laid her down easily to the ground and stood up looking at Fahd. He approached him slowly and Fahd started to stand up. Hazem continued to watch Fahd carefully and to point the gun at him.

Fadi told Fahd: Less than an hour ago I was an animal like you. But now, I can no longer bring myself to kill. Jesus has washed all hatred out of my heart. It is due to this good woman that you just murdered, that I will not kill you. I will never kill again. Go on your way. I pray that God's mercy will reach you someday. Even a heart as dark as yours can be changed. Not by me or by any man, but by God's love and God's grace. Go away from here. I can't guarantee what will happen to you if other villagers come here after hearing the shots. They will surely kill you. Fadi then reached to the table and took what bread remained and threw it in a sack along with some dried figs that were hung on the wall and gave the sack to Fahd.

Fahd looked at him, then at Hazem and the gun. He finally gazed down upon Umm George and his face suddenly darkened. He looked sorrowfully at Fadi and said: I did not mean to kill her. Those bullets were meant for you. You are now an apostate and it is my duty to kill you. Don't think that a few loaves of bread and figs will change that. If I see you again, you will not find any mercy in me.

Hazem said: You better go now before I lose my self-control and shoot you down like the dog that you are. I will not shed blood here in Umm George's home, but if I see you somewhere else, I will not hesitate to drag you to the nearest Kataeb band and let them deal with you. Leave and don't ever come back.

With that, Fahd turned his head and looked at Fadi with a smirk on his face and said: I am sure that we will meet again. He turned his back to both of them and ran down the road with the sack held tightly in his hand.

Chapter 11

Layla was now thinking about Rose again. Most people called her Umm George, but Layla liked the name Rose better. It made her think of how lively and beautiful and fragrant Umm George's life was. She loved her with all her heart. The day she heard about her murder she was shocked. She could not believe that anyone would be evil enough to kill such a loving and gentle and generous woman. She treated everyone as if they were her own children. She never complained or said discouraging remarks. Never tired of doing good for others and giving of what little she had to others.

Why do good people have to die like that? First was George, then Rose.

It was Elias her distant cousin that brought the news to her. She and Feliep went to the village that same day for her burial. It was there that she saw Fadi again. It had been at least three years prior to that since she saw him last. She heard of the changes that happened to him, that he became a fighter and that he had killed many people. She could not believe that the gentle, sensitive little boy that held a dying dove in his hands and was crying for it like a little baby, could become a heartless murderer.

When she saw him there, her heart jumped. He was handsome as ever. She always liked the way he looked. Wild looking but clean and slim. She saw a little child whenever she looked into his wandering eyes. That day she saw pain and grief.

Her brother wanted to kill him. He told her that he had killed Saleem and that he had changed. He was no longer the boy she knew in her childhood, or the young man they went to school with.

Hazem was there however, and he told them about how Fadi came to Rose's house and the events that took place and how Rose died defending him.

Feliep could care less. He was still determined to kill Fadi. Hazem had to watch him closely throughout the burial ceremony and prayers and the next two days they were there.

Fadi stayed in a room with Hazem. He did not eat or drink for the next two days. He spent the next two days mostly on his knees praying and sobbing. He had Rose's bible with him, and he was reading it almost non-stop. Hazem tried to bring him food and water, but he rejected that completely. He asked to be left alone to grief and to pour his heart before God and pour his heart he did. He confessed before God all the sins he could remember. He cried repeatedly for the killing of Saleem which he had never forgotten. He Asked God for forgiveness and promised to follow Jesus wherever he led him. He read in the gospel of John "I am the gate; whoever enters through me will be saved. They will come in and go out, and find pasture"

He also read: "I am the good shepherd. The good shepherd lays down his life for the sheep. The hired hand is not the shepherd and does not own the sheep. So, when he sees the wolf coming, he abandons the sheep and runs away. Then the wolf attacks the flock and scatters it. The man runs away because he is a hired hand and cares nothing for the sheep. I am the good shepherd; I know my sheep and my sheep know me just as the Father knows me and I know the Father—and I lay down my life for the sheep."

He ate the words up. He was so hungry and thirsty for the word of God that he could not stop reading and praying. Despite his grief for Umm George, he was experiencing peace and true joy for the first time in his life.

This was not an earthly type of joy that can disappear with the changing of the circumstances of life. Nor was this the sort of joy that was superficial, but a very deep joy such as a river rushing out of his own soul. It was overwhelming.

He continued to pray and as he did so, his prayers changed from prayers of repentance to prayers of gratitude, thankfulness, praise and worship to God the father, Jesus the son and the Holy Spirit.

It was at the end of his two days of fasting that he finally left the room and came back to the main house. Feliep and Layla and Hazem were all sitting around the table drinking tea with mint leaves.

Fadi came into the room, and he was radiant. His face looked tired, and his hair was oily and disheveled, but there was an unmistakable assurance and joy showing in his eyes and face.

He sat down at the table and asked for food. Hazem brought him some olive oil and Za'atar, white cheese and butter with some bread and poured a cup of tea for him.

He was very hungry now and he ate while the others talked. Once in a while, Layla would glance at him, and he would catch her glance and his face would turn red.

He had not seen Layla for several years. He could not visit her anymore and tried very hard not to think about her after he started his Jihad. To him she was forbidden, an infidel.

He did not remember when his feelings about her had changed. He loved her since the day he met her. Yet after the war started and he had blood on his hands, he could not bring himself to think about her. It is not that he stopped loving her, more so that he thought her to be too pure to be in his thoughts along with all the other thoughts of hate and violence. Now he is happy to see her. He wanted to tell her that he became a different person, that he was …born again, that he is a new man now. He felt clean and guilt free for the first time in his life and suddenly as if he was a child again, he regained his innocence.

Layla was afraid to look at him much due to her brother. He was angry enough without her making matters worse. He had heard the story that Hazem told, and he was not convinced. He said that Moslems don't change. That Fadi was playing some kind of game and shouldn't be trusted.

Hazem told him: Feliep, you have known me for a while now. Have I been playing a game too? I too was a Moslem then came to know Christ. I have been faithful to my belief in Jesus and have followed his teachings. Can you tell me if I have at any time given you reason to doubt my sincerity?

-You are different Hazem. We know you and trust you, but Fadi…

-Fadi is a new man. He has been reborn by the Spirit of God and washed clean by the blood of Jesus. He is more of a Christian now than many who call themselves Christians yet do all sort of things that Christ abhors.

-Well, I hope so. That would make me happy. It is just that I can't forget that he killed Saleem our friend from school for no cause at all. I suppose that if God wants to give him a second chance, then who am I to say no. As long as he stays away from me and my sister. We will be leaving tomorrow anyway. Be careful Hazem and don't trust him too much.

Chapter 12

It was early March in 1978 and the days were starting to warm up nicely in Southern Lebanon. South of the Litani River the Christian Militia led by Maj. Saad Haddad had significant control over this sector. There were many Palestinian fighters in the area however and they continued to attack targets in Southern Lebanon and even in Northern Israel. It was guerilla warfare and PLO fighters were experts at this type of war. Their hit and run tactics, kidnappings and bombing of targets had been very effective. Their activities recently have intensified. Maj. Haddad's army had not been able to stop them or slow them down much. Israel now was becoming very irritated and Israeli citizens living close to the Southern Lebanese border had been hit hard repeatedly. They urged their government for action.

Syrian troops were now occupying Beqaa Valley at 50,000 strong. They started by shelling Palestinian camps and fighters, then turned around and started pushing back Christian Kataeb militias who did not like the presence of Syria in Lebanon. They understood that Syria always considered Lebanon as part of Greater Syria and therefore were possibly looking to gain control over Lebanon. The Lebanese Kataeb and the smaller less effective Lebanese army attempted to block their advance.

In all this mess, Iran added to the mixture of Chaos by sending fighters into Lebanon to help the Shiites in Southern Lebanon and to counterbalance the SLA (Southern Lebanese Army) led by Maj.

Haddad. These fighters were small in numbers initially and trickled into Lebanon un-noticed, slowly adding to the strength of the Shiites.

Daoud came into the tent of his regiment's commanding office and gave a military solute. He was a young man in his early 20s. He has been serving his mandatory military service in the IDF for over 3 years now. He was an engineering student, and he was assigned to a technical unit in the IDF.

Rav sirin (Major) Gilad told him to stand at ease then asked him for his report

Daoud reported: We are ready to cross the Litani River if indicated. The water level is acceptable. We have arranged for mobile bridges and amphibious vehicles.

-Good job Daoud. You have been reliable.

-Thank you, Sir,

-We have had reports that a gruesome terrorist attack had just taken place. Several Palestinian fighters led by a woman hijacked two buses near Haifa and took the coastal road into Tel Aviv. We finally got them but not before they killed over 30 and wounded over 70 of our people.

-That is terrible sir. These constant attacks must be stopped. The militants must be driven out of Southern Lebanon.

Maj. Gilad said: They should all be driven out. We are going in with about 25,000 troops and our aim is to mop up Southern Lebanon. We will most likely go north of the Litani River. We need as much water as possible for our lands and our people. The Litani would be a nice acquisition

-But…forgive me for saying this Sir, aren't we forcing people out of their lands and homes if we do this. I mean, all we should be doing is pushing back the PLO fighters and militants, but to drive people out of their homes is not right. It was done to us and we didn't like it. Now we are doing it to others!

-Daoud you are still young and naïve. You can't drive these PLO dogs out of Southern Lebanon without also driving out all who may support them. That is why we are backing up Maj. Saad Haddad. We are hoping that his Christian militia will control Southern Lebanon and create a buffer zone between us and the PLO. Let Arabs then fight it out among themselves. I don't care if they all kill each other. The more dead the better. That will only leave less of them for us to kill later. Don't think that we will stop at the Litani. Our objective is not only to drive the PLO out, but also to drive the Syrian dogs back into their country.

-It seems to me that killing will only lead to more killing Sir. I mean, I am a loyal Israeli and a good Jew. But I cannot approve of what we did in recent months in South Lebanon. We massacred innocent people. Women and children were among those massacred heartlessly. How could we do this after what was done to us in Europe and Germany. Aren't we repeating the same atrocities that we suffered ourselves?

-Be careful of what you are saying Daoud. I like you, but don't like what I am hearing from you now. You worry about their women and children? Don't forget that their women feed their children hate for us along with breast milk, and don't forget that their children will one day become fighters that will come after me and you, our mothers and sisters. I tell you Daoud, in war there is no mercy. It is survival of the fittest. Kill or be killed.

-Forgive me Sir, but I believe that human beings are capable of behaving better than that. We are more vicious than animals. Killing should never become so easy no matter who the enemy is. We must always remember that we too were once weak and persecuted. How can we now become the persecutors? I feel that we are going too far.

-In fact Daoud we have not gone far enough yet. If it was up to me I would Napalm all of Southern Lebanon and purify it from all those dirty Arabs. We can't be weak. Remember what happened to us in Europe. We swore that we will never let anybody push us around anymore. It's an eye for an eye and a tooth for a tooth.

-Yes Sir. I just don't like us massacring women and children. I also don't like us supporting that renegade Major Haddad. I don't like his tactics and don't trust him at all.

-Our government trusts him and sees the potential in him to be a strong ally. We have been arming him and his men heavily. Our leadership is using him as a surrogate Israeli force. He can be used very effectively to do things we can't do without bringing international retribution. He is Lebanese and can always claim that he is a revolutionary fighting for the freedom of his country. He is our dog and he will bite our enemies in the butt when needed. Now, be dismissed and get yourself and your men ready. The attack will begin at 03:00 hour.

Daoud saluted his superior then turned around and left the tent. He flagged a jeep and ordered the driver to take him to his command post. Rav samal (Chief Sergeant) Ariel his second in command was standing over the maps and making some measurements. When he saw Daoud he stood in attention and saluted.

Daoud said: Are we ready Ariel. The attack will begin at 03:00. We need to go over the attack plans carefully. Our movements must be coordinated perfectly. There is no room for error.

Ariel answered: Yes Sir, understood Sir. I have gone over the plans carefully. Our equipment is ready. The troops understand the plan of action very well. I personally went over it with all squad leaders. We will have our victory Sir.

-Yes Ariel, I believe that we will. I just hope that this incursion will not cause many fatalities and that civilians will be spared this time.

-Collateral damage is inevitable Sir. War has its costs and tragedies. We can't let a few civilian casualties prevent us from protecting our people from daily bombardment by Palestinian guerilla fighters. Northern Israel must become safe.

-To us they are just a few casualties but remember that they have families and people who love them. It is enough that they live in the most miserable of conditions. Remember that we drove them out of their lands and homes. Now we mean to annihilate them. I fear the judgment of God if we continue this road.

-Permission to speak freely Sir

-Permission granted

-Sir, where was God when we were being burned in the gas chambers and slaughtered like pigs. Where was he when Jewish families were ripped a part. Where was he when women were raped in front of their husbands and children and fathers beaten and shot in front of their wives and children? Where was our God when we were being experimented on like animals and imprisoned in camps and used like trash? We are called his chosen people and that's why he punishes us when we stray away from him! Well Sir, I wish that he would choose some other people once in a while. We have been tormented throughout history. Time for us to stand on our own and protect ourselves.

-Look Ariel, my family and I lived in Lebanon all our lives before the state of Israel was formed. We then made "aliyah" to Israel. When we were living in Lebanon, we never had any problems with anyone. Our neighbors treated us as their own. We went to all their weddings and funerals, and they came to ours. My mother used to spend every morning with our neighbor Regina drinking Arabic coffee and gossiping. I played with Raimone and Enri her children all the time. I went to school as a kid and was never ostracized or ridiculed. We were happy.

Not all Arabs hate Jews. We lived in peace with Arabs for hundreds of years. We were treated much better by them than we were treated by the Europeans. We had the same rights of citizenship that they had. We had our shops and businesses and even high-ranking government jobs. Now we are hated because of this war. Sometimes I think that we would have been better off had the state of Israel not been established.

-Sir, that is dangerous thinking. Many in the army are staunch Zionists. Your comments may get you into some serious trouble.

-Ariel, my beliefs are not unique. Many Hassidic Rabbis and many religious Jews believe that the state of Israel was formed outside the will of God. We are forbidden by the Three Oaths to go back to Israel in mass. You should read Rabbi Teitelbaum's thoughts on the matter. He is the leader of over 100,000 Haredi Orthodox Jews. He is a scholar of great weight, and his opinions can't be taken lightly. He, among many others believe that the forming of the state of Israel and Zionism are at the root of all the problems that we are facing as Jews. As a matter of fact, most Zionists are atheists and reject teachings of the Torah and do not keep Mitzvah.

-Sir, are you saying that you don't believe in our right to exist as a nation?!

-No Ariel. I don't agree with Rabbi Teitelbaum, but I certainly understand where he is coming from. I just look at the way we have been living since 1948 and I don't see how this is a good thing. I believe in peace whenever possible. I am a soldier however, and I will do my best to make sure that if we fight a war, we win it.

-You had me going there for a minute Sir. I thought I had to report you to Rasan Gilad.

-Gilad would have executed me on the spot. I have never met anyone with so much hate and disgust as he has. I would hate to be his enemy.

They both laughed loudly and went back to the charts to discuss the plans one more time.

Chapter 13

Layla and her brother went back to Beirut a few days after the funeral. She was still in shock for Rose dying in such a way. She never expected her to be killed. Even in dying, she saved a life. That was Rose. Always giving of herself to others. She had been a great teacher to Layla.

She was also amazed at Fadi. She had given hope up on him since he became a fighter and shot Saleem. Everyone in the village, including their Moslem neighbors hated him for that vicious act. They could not believe that he shot down his own friend in cold blood. Yet, that is what religious extremism does to a person. It blinds a person completely.

Last time she saw Fadi prior to this was over four years ago. They met together by the small brook by the apple and plum fields. He asked her to meet him there for a very important reason. He wanted to tell her that he was joining a group of Fedayeen (sworn martyrs).

She was surprised by his news. They had known each other by then for several years. They had become very close. She even had a fuzzy, warm feeling for him whenever she thought of him. She could not spend a day without thinking about him. He also had told her that she was the only person in his life that made him happy. He said that whenever they were together, he felt as if the whole world was happy too. He held her hand in his on that day and looked down as he told her. He was unable to look her in the eye. She put her left hand on his cheek and tried to turn his face towards her, but he would not.

She finally saw a tear trickle down his cheek. She asked him why he would do such a thing. Why he would intentionally leave her, and worse, fight in a war that was wrong and evil by all accounts.

Fadi told her: My uncle had been talking to me lately. He also brought with him a friend that had been fighting Jihad for the last 10 years. They read to me from the Quran and talked to me about my duties as a Moslem man. They said that there is no cause higher than the cause of fighting for Allah.

She told him that he was a good man already. She reminded him of how much they have helped the less fortunate. How they used to go together to Palestinian camps and take food, blankets and sweets with them to give to the people. She reminded him how he always helped the elderly in the village and did many chores for them without accepting any form of payment. She reminded him how he used to go to church with her sometimes and light candles and repeat the prayers.

She held on tightly to his hand and told him that Allah would not want him to kill other people just because they didn't believe the way he did. She tried to convince him and change his mind about going to war, but he would not budge. Finally, he withdrew his hand quickly from hers, kissed her a very short kiss on the cheek and told her that he loved her, then went up the hill and disappeared.

Since that day she heard many stories about him. He had become a well-known fighter. People in the village talked about skirmishes he had with Israelis and Druz and Kataeb. He never joined the PLO but sided with them and fought many battles at their side.

When the news about how he killed Saleem came to her, she almost fainted. She could not believe that he had turned so dark. She could not eat for three days. She became depressed and everyone knew the reason why. The entire village knew that Fadi and Layla were in love. No one minded that they were a Christian and a Moslem in love with each other. After the war however, all that had changed. Everything became centered on what a person's religion or political affiliation was. People were shot in cold blood over that. No other reason was needed to kill a person other than belonging to the wrong group.

Now that she saw him again, all these memories came back. She was so happy to see that he had become a Christian. That he asked for forgiveness and gave his life to Christ. She knew that he would be a faithful follower. That all his zeal and courage would now be used to help others. Her heart suddenly filled with joy. She lifted her eyes to heaven and said: Thank you Jesus. Thank you, Aunt Rose.

She can dream about him again. She can dream about marriage and life and children. She can hope for a peaceful Lebanon. If Fadi can change, then so can others. God is able to bring peace to this land.

Now she needed to see her own brother change his ways. He too had become a fighter and had joined Al Kataeb militias. He would disappear from home for several weeks at a time. He had become a fierce warrior. She heard stories of him storming into Palestinian buildings and bunkers and demolishing them. He would crawl into the sewers carrying TNT and place explosives underneath enemy unit headquarters and blow them up.

She had warned him and begged him to stop. She told him that Jesus taught against violence. That he loved the whole world and gave his life for all, Moslems as well as Christians. He taught us to love and forgive our enemies and that all who live by the sword shall die by the sword.

He used to laugh at her. He would say: religion is religion and politics is politics. You can't mix them together. We can't let these Palestinian dogs take our beautiful Lebanon. It is not our fault that they lost their land. We gave them homes and allowed them into our country, and now they want to take it over. You know that they were forming roadblocks and stopping Lebanese citizens and asking for their IDs and then shooting them on site if they had Christian names. How can we let them treat us like this when it's our country and they are refugees here?

She would tell him: You can't blame all Palestinians and Moslems for that. Many are still our good neighbors and love us and we love them. Don't become a murderer. God will judge you for every bad deed you will do. You are not defending Lebanon when you join a militia. You are only adding to the violence and chaos. But he would not listen. His anger seems to have been fueled once more now that he saw Fadi again. He did not want his only beloved sister to be married to a Moslem, even if he converted.

When they got to their apartment in Beirut, he told her to lock everything up and not open the door for anyone. She knew that her brother will use the signal they agreed upon whenever he came to the apartment. He always worried about her and she about him. He would always keep the apartment well stocked with food and drink. He had drums of water filled to the rim to be used for cooking and washing in case the municipal water supply was depleted or cut off. He had plenty of canned tuna and beef and Halawa as well as olives, makdous and other sundries.

She on the other hand could only pray for him whenever he left on one of his missions.

This time he did not come back on his own two feet. He was carried back to her by two of his friends. He was attempting to demolish a building known to hide many Palestinian fighters. He set the explosives in the sewers beneath the building, but the fuse was too short. The TNT exploded while he was still there. The explosion burned a good portion of his face and blinded him. Fragments of metal and other shrapnel cut through his side and thighs and back. When he was brought back to her, he was delirious and barely conscious.

She kept him in the apartment since then. She had been cleaning his wounds and dressing them daily. She never left his side since his injuries except to get him medicine.

She wished that Fadi was here to help her. He could have eased her burden and talked to her brother. They could get to know each other again and hopefully Feliep would forgive him. She loved them both and wanted them both in her life. That would be very hard, but she believed in a God that can change people's hearts.

Chapter 14

Lila sat down beside her living room window looking down at the street. This used to be a very clean street filled with the noise of people talking and laughing, and sometimes cursing loudly, and the noise of cars beeping their horns with the drivers occasionally extending their hands out of their driver-side windows in obscene gestures and screaming curses and profanities. Something for which Lebanese people are so famous for. Now the street became almost empty with a casual passerby moving quickly and looking from side to side as if expecting to be hit by a bullet or a piece of shrapnel at any time. The street was littered with empty cartridge shells, pieces of concrete and glass, torn papers and magazines, and here and there a bloody piece of bone shrapnel or decayed flesh.

She cried and her tears felt very warm on her cheeks. She couldn't believe the destruction that her beloved city and neighborhood had experienced. She couldn't fathom the spilling of innocent blood and the killing of innocent people both old and young. What has happened to her Beirut? The Lovely maiden sitting by the sea. The Paris of the Middle East. The ever awake, ever lively city full of lights and people from all over the world living and eating, drinking and laughing in peace. What happened to the morning visits and the sharing of stories and gossip on the balconies over coffee? What happened to evenings filled with music and people and visitors eating Tabbouli and Kebbi Nayye and drinking Araq? What happened to the voices of Sabah and Fairouz filling the streets over loudspeakers as people went by humming along with the melodies.

This now is a very different city. A city filled with hatred and blood. An evil unlike any she had ever seen before has gripped this city with deadly fingers of death and destruction. An evil that is overwhelming in proportion. A veil of darkness had fallen over Lebanon and secluded the light. A suffocating sense of helplessness and tragedy has now completely prevailed over all in Lebanon.

She wiped away her tears and took a very deep sigh and went into her brother's room. He was in his bed as usual. Eyes closed with bandages. Arms and neck covered with terrible burns. A bandage on his left side was bloody and wet.

-Philiep, Philiep habibi, can you hear me.

A moan came out and was hardly discernible.

She started to weep again. How her brother lived through the explosion nobody could tell. But he did not come out of it unscathed. He had earned the scars of war now, both the visible ones, and the much more severe ones that nobody can see.

She called out her brother's name again and did not get an answer.

She sat beside him quietly and started to clean his burns. This is a procedure that she has been doing over the last three months. His burns had gotten much better with her tender care, yet his site had not returned and the burns on his eye lids and forehead had scarred him in an ugly fashion and changed forever the handsome face of her beloved younger brother.

She poured the Saline solution over the gauze and gently washed off his burned skin. Loose pieces of skin and thick brownish drainage came off. She continued to wash and clean his arms and neck. She took the Silvadene cream and started to paste his burns with it, then covered his arms and neck with thick white gauze. He did not even stir. She knew that he was in pain but did not want her to know. She kept silent and went on to change the dressing on his side. This is the area that has been giving him even more trouble than his burns. It continued to drain heavily, and sometimes fresh bleeding could be seen. She touched the bandage and started to remove the tape holding it to his side. He jerked quickly to the other side and winced in pain. She immediately put her hand over his head and kissed him by his ear and whispered to him to be strong. She continued to remove the bandage. His wound looked deep and ugly. Thick shrapnel was removed from that wound. It was done here at home by a nurse who was acting as a surgeon during the war. There were not enough doctors or surgeons left to treat the wounded. Those who were not killed, ran off. Few stayed behind to help their countrymen. Those who stayed behind did not have the proper instruments and materials needed anymore and people had to find what was needed on their own. Those people who had any type of medical knowledge picked up the slack. Many people died under their care even though they did their best. With time, however, they learned more and more and became at least efficient enough to save some lives. Her brother's life among those saved.

-Hold on Philiep, I will be done in no time at all.

A mixture of a grin and a grimace came over his face as he said,

-Your hands have been blessed by the Virgin Mary. They are compassionate and have the powers of healing within them. I don't know how long I am going to keep causing you this aggravation. You need to leave Beirut and go to the village. It is up in the mountains and much safer than here.

-Shsh, I told you that I will not leave you here to die. You can't be moved, and I will stay beside you till you heal. No more ignorant talk about me leaving and going to the village. What am I going to do there anyway? Milk the cows or bake bread. You know that I am not fit for such work. I will stay here in Beirut with you and whatever happens, let it happen.

-But…, Philiep said, and she quieted him again as she continued to wash then pack and dress his wound. She noticed that the area around his wound had become intensely red and that streaks of redness were going up his side. His whole side felt as if it was on fire. She checked his forehead with her hand, and it felt very hot. She asked him if he had any chills at night and he answered her that he was shaking most of the night in his bed with chills but did not want to wake her up.

She lifted her head up to heaven and said: Ya Adra Mariam (O Virgin Mary). She was very worried now. All the antibiotic capsules she had were gone. There were no more, and no place to get any. All the pharmacies had been looted. She was unable to reach anyone in the black market anymore after her cousin Clouvis disappeared and no one knew where he was anymore or whether he was alive or dead.

She knew that her brother's condition was very bad and worsening by the day. He was having more frequent fevers, and she once saw him shake in bed so hard she thought he was having a seizure.

She must somehow get her hands on some antibiotics, or her beloved brother will die. She had to find a way to get them.

-Philiep, I will be back soon. I am just going over to the other side of the street to Aunt Marie to see if she is ok.

-Please don't go. I don't want my angel to go back to heaven yet. Please don't go.

-I will be fine. Adra Mariam will watch over me. You just wait and I will be back sooner than you think.

She put on her shawl and shoes and took with her a bracelet that her mom had given her years ago. It was 21 Karat gold and weighed 140 grams. It should get her some more antibiotics if she can find a buyer. No matter what happens, she must try. She came out of the apartment and quickly locked the door then went down the stairway now littered with bottles and refuse till she reached the ground level. She looked around and saw no one. She slowly eased her way out of the main door and ducked quickly into the street and disappeared around the corner of the building and into the chaos of the city.

Chapter · 15

Hazem and Fadi now had no place to go. After Rose was buried and Layla and Feliep left to Beirut, her home was shut down until her inheritance could be divided among her survivors. Since her only son died and she was a widow, her relatives had to file for inheritance. The government, however, was no longer functioning due to the war and her house was simply locked up and boarded.

Hazem and Fadi took some food with them and took the shot gun for protection against wild animals but broke the Kalashnikov into pieces and threw the ammunition down the well. They both had knives with them and took some matches and rope.

They headed south. They made a pact with each other to fight this war in a different way. They were going to join a medical unit and care for the wounded. They were also intent on bringing food and clean water into the camps. At this point, the Palestinian camps were mostly isolated and were being shelled regularly. Their intention was to bring aid to them and to other needy areas.

They had to find transportation. They could not walk all the way to the camps. Hazem suggested that they walk along the main road and try to flag someone going south towards the camps. Fadi agreed.

They walked for several hours till they got to the main road leading from the village to Beirut and then started going in a Southwest direction for approximately 2 more hours. They rarely saw traffic. A jeep with three armed men passed them by. They hid behind some trees when they heard the jeep coming. The men appeared to be Kataeb militiamen. An hour later a lone man on a motorcycle passed them by. He was weaving back and forth on the road and did not seem to be in control of his machine. He had a Soloug wrapped around his head. They saw a huge red spot on his right shoulder and right side as he passed them by. Less than a minute passed by when they heard a crash and a loud agonizing scream just ahead. They both ran down the road and found the motorcycle on its side still spinning its wheels. The man was lying on his back and groaning. He was thrown off the motorcycle to the side of the road and landed on some soft brush. They both rushed to him. His face was caked with blood and a large hole was in the right side of his leather vest from an apparent bullet that had penetrated his right shoulder. This explained the huge red spot on the back of his shoulder that they saw when he passed them by earlier. There was fresh bleeding from the wound now. He appeared to be in shock. He was cursing and praying at the same time. When Fadi approached him, the man looked at him with empty eyes, clutched Fadi's right arm with his trembling left hand and asked him if he was an enemy or a friend. Fadi looked at Hazem, then turned his head back to the man and told him that he was a friend. He told him not to talk and tried to get his vest off. The man clutched harder to his arm and shook his head. He said: Don't even bother. I am gone. I bled too much. I can hardly feel my limbs now and I know I have very little time. Listen, in my left vest pocket is some money, a picture of my wife and a letter I wrote to her but never could get it over to her. Her name is Alia, she is in Al Nabatieh camp in the South with her family. I have not been able to get to her. I am a Lebanese Mourani and she is a Palestinian who was studying in Beirut. I met her in Jonieh and we fell in love. We married before the war. We got separated when all the trouble began and she went south to Al Nabatieh to her family. We thought it would be safer for her there. I was wrong. Please take this to her. It is all my savings. He squeezed Fadi's hand and said: May God protect those you love. His grip then slowly relaxed and his eyes rolled backwards, and he passed.

Fadi could not help himself but cry. The death of Umm George was still fresh in his mind and heart, and this man's death brought to the surface deep welled up feelings. He rubbed his eyes in an effort not to cry. Hazem was already crying. It is a tragedy beyond understanding how human life can so easily be wasted. They knew that they were both guilty in their past of doing some horrendous things. They knew that they had caused so much pain to so many people. They knelt together before the dead man and said a prayer for him and for his loved ones. They searched his vest pocket and took out the money, letter and several small pictures of what appeared to be his father and mother, possibly some siblings and a picture of what they thought must be Alia. They wrapped everything together with a piece of cloth and Fadi pocketed the package. They dug a grave and buried the man.

Hazem went over to the motorcycle and picked it up. It did not appear to be badly damaged. He tested it. All the mechanisms worked. There were only dents and scratches on the body of it but no mechanical damage. He started it again and Fadi got on the seat behind him, and they started south again towards the Palestinian camps and towards Nabetieh.

They drove for about three hours. They were shot at once by a sniper who was hiding behind some pine trees. They never saw him, but saw a flash then heard the bullet as it kicked asphalt right to their left. They kept on going south. They had their story ready. They have fought along- side the PLO and knew some of the fighters. They were known at some of the cafés along the road to Nebatieh. Fadi used to go often to Ein El-Helwi and Rashidieh and some of the smaller camps with Layla to bring food and supplies. They knew him and respected him down there. He would have no trouble once he was in the south.

They stopped in Jezzine and had something to eat. They looked like everybody else. No differentiating marks or clothes. They had only their shot gun for a weapon, but that was not an assault weapon, and it was recognized as such. They drew no attention to themselves. They ate and had tea with mint leaves afterwards, then left.

It was nighttime now but they pressed on. They kept on going till they reached the camp at midnight. They did not enter the camp zone. They stayed on the outskirts and decided to sleep and enter in the morning. A case of mistaken identity could result in them being killed without mercy. They did not have any blankets. They lay down by the trunk of an old walnut tree and pulled their jackets around themselves as much as possible and curled up and slept. They did not dare light a fire. They kept the motorcycle in between themselves. The motor was still very hot, and it gave some heat which helped them go to sleep. Throughout the night they would wake to the sounds of howling and due to the deep chill, that pierced their bones.

Chapter 16

Layla was quick and very careful. She dove in between the torn down buildings and rubble and ducked here and ran there. There were no bullets aimed at her and she saw no fighters, but that was the problem. It wasn't the fighters that she could see that worried her. She could always outsmart or avoid those. It was the snipers that caused her worry. They did not care who they shot at. They shot down men, women and children in cold blood. They were merciless and they were accurate.

She thought that if they shot her, she wouldn't even know it. She would be dead before she hit the ground.

She had to get to the Northern part of the city. There was a man there who had everything. He had relatives in Syria, and he would make regular trips there. He would come back with a car full of medicines, batteries, canned and dried foods, sweets, clothes and everything else you could think of. Her brother needed antibiotics, or he would die. She had to get him medication at any cost.

She was looking far to her right, towards the top floor of the nearest building. She thought she saw a flash of something. As she continued forward, she stepped on a loose stone and her right ankle twisted. She immediately fell to her right side and as she did so, a shower of dust and small fragments of rock hit her left side as a bullet hit the wall she was walking beside. She covered her eyes immediately and she screamed in pain and fear as she felt stinging pain from her face and neck. The bullet had just missed her head. She did not even hear the sound till after she was hit. She quickly checked her surroundings. Thanked God that she fell behind some rubble that was about a meter or so in height. She was completely hidden from the sniper's view if she stayed down. She started checking herself now. There was some bleeding from her face and neck, but not serious. The small fragments of rock must have caused some damage to her skin. Her eyes were not harmed, and she sighed and thanked God again. She looked down at her right ankle and was terrified to see how swollen it had gotten in a matter of only a few minutes. She could not move her ankle at all. The pain from her ankle was agonizing. She thought she may have broken it.

She trembled in fear. How is she going to get the medicine for her brother now? How is she even going to get back home?

She did not hear any sounds, and no more bullets were fired. The sniper must have thought that he hit her and that she was badly injured or dead, else he would have fired again. If she can stay here till dark, she can ease her way back home hiding behind the rubble and broken-down walls without anyone noticing her.

She sat there with her hands covering her face and started to sob. What will happen to Philiep now? How is he going to get the medications that he needs. Is he awake and asking for her now, or is he wondering if she had abandoned him?

What about her. She can't leave her hiding place till dusk or even dark. Any movement before that may attract the attention of the sniper and this time he may not miss. If she stayed here too long however, the dogs might get her. There were no dogs in Beirut not that long ago. After the war started and bodies of dead people littered the streets, packs of dogs started to show up in the streets. They were hungry and vicious, and they had tasted human blood. They would tear her apart if they got a hold of her. If she was lucky enough to escape the dogs, she may fall prey to the other wild animals that patrolled the streets at night. They were fighters from different factions, and they too were looking for human blood.

Death, destruction and inhumanity were now normal parts of daily living in Beirut.

Chapter 17

Layla's ankle continued to swell and hurt. She knew that she had to get home and put some ice on her ankle and splint it. She must have slept for a while for it was dusk now and some fires were being built. She could not see the fires but could smell the aroma of burning wood in the air. She looked around and did not see any movement, nor did she hear any alarming sounds. She stood carefully from behind her wall of debris and looked around again. She saw no movement. She gathered herself and stood halfway up to test her strength. She was in severe pain and her right ankle and foot felt numb, but she was able to maintain her balance. She knew she had to get home as soon as possible. She turned around and started running with her head held low. She ignored the pain shooting through her leg and kept on going as fast as she could until she disappeared into a side street. There she went through several torn down buildings then turned south and continued running biting her lips due to pain till she got to her street. She then slowed down a little bit and took a deep breath. She looked down at her right leg and was astonished by how swollen it was. It looked like a light pole. Her ankle was not distinguishable from the rest of her leg. The whole leg was one thickness, and all curves and contours were completely lost. Bluish discoloration was seen on both sides of her ankle.

She had to get home as soon as possible. She bit her lips again and ran towards her building. When she arrived, she opened the outer door quickly and ducked inside in a flash. She shot up the stairs to her apartment and opened the door. By now she was in complete agony.

She wanted to scream from pain. Hot searing pain has taken over her entire right leg. She could hardly stand on it now. She immediately went to the ice box and got some ice. She wrapped the ice in a towel and tied the towel to her right ankle then sat down and elevated her foot over a chair and two pillows. She took a long deep sigh, put her head back and slowly started to cry.

Philiep yelled out to her: Layla, is that you? Where were you? Are you alright? How's aunt? Why did you take so long?

-All is fine Philiep. Aunt is doing well. I will be with you very soon. I just have to wash up first. Don't worry.

-Alright, maybe we can talk a little bit after you're done. I would like to hear about what's going on outside.

Layla: sure, I will be right there.

She went back to the kitchen and washed her face, wiping away the tears. She swallowed four Aspirins. He must not find out what happened. She must keep the horrors of what is happening outside away from him. He has enough pain and did not need any more worries. She has to get antibiotics for him, or she may lose him to infection and fever. Suddenly a stab of pain went through her chest and her stomach sank. She thought that if anything happened to her younger brother, she would die. She couldn't imagine life without her brother, the only family she had left.

She lifted her head up and started praying:

"Ya Massieh (Oh Christ), help me take care of him and get him his medicine. Give me the strength that I need to help him. I know that if you wanted him dead, he wouldn't be here by now. You must still have some purpose for his life. Please forgive him for all that he has done. Give him enough days to make things right with you".

Tears streamed down her cheeks, but she felt much better. She knew that despite all her failures God still listened to her. He was ever-present around her and in her heart and within her very being since the day she knelt before him and surrendered her life to him. Oh; she was not especially sinful. She hasn't done anything really bad ever. She was kind to people and gentle with animals. She never intentionally hurt anyone. Yet she always felt very insecure regarding her relationship with God. Her insecurity stemmed from the fact that she knew she was unworthy of God's love. Although she went to church often with her parents and fasted every Wednesday and Friday, and observed religious holidays and duties, yet she felt separated from God. All the religious activities she participated in were superficial and did not diminish her guilt and feelings of unworthiness. Yet she yearned in her heart for peace and absolution.

Her sins were instinctive. Rarely did she knowingly plan on doing something bad. She did some vengeful things to other schoolgirls and to her cousin once out of jealousy, but the majority of her moral failures were unplanned and a natural response to events.

She would get furious when anyone criticized her and inside her heart, she would wish all sorts of bad things to happen to them. She was very quick to anger. She remembers how envious of others she every time would be she saw someone having something she wished for herself. She remembers how she wished Nadia, her neighbor, would fall and break her neck when she saw her riding that beautiful pony one time. She remembers how she tried to feed her pony grass laced with Epsom salts in order to give it diarrhea. The pony almost died, and nobody knew that she did it. She remembers how she stole apples from their neighbor's orchard and how one day she spat in a glass of water before bringing it to Umm Nabil, their heavy-set neighbor who gossiped so much and whom she disliked.

Things like that were mostly impulsive and were done without planning. She was, however, capable of planning evil deeds when the necessity arose.

She did that one time when her mother killed two white doves to make a meal for a visitor that came unexpectedly from town. She loved those two doves and would watch them all the time as they flew back and forth to their nest. She was so mad at her mother and the visitor that she wanted to get back at them. Their visitor spent the night at their home. She stayed late at night thinking of ways to have her revenge. She woke up early next morning and sneaked into the guest room. She took away his pants and went to the stables and wiped them on the urine and dung. She took them back to his room and then went back to sleep as if nothing had ever happened. She woke up a short while later to see her mom slapping her thighs with her hands and then slapping her cheeks and running to heat up water to wash their guest's pants. He remained in the guest room till the afternoon and refused to have breakfast or lunch. She felt very satisfied with what she had done.

As she became older however, she started to think seriously about her life. When her mother passed away, she was only 16 years old. Her father then married another woman only 6 months after her mother died. She was a very good and compassionate woman, but she was not her Mom. She started wondering about where her mom was. She knew that there is a heaven, but how could she be sure that her mom was there. She loved her mom so much, she wanted to be with her. It was that year that she started to change. Her happiness perished and her spunkiness had died with the death of her mother. She suddenly became timid and docile. Then she became depressed. Then she became suicidal.

Chapter · 18

Layla wiped away her tears. She must tend to her brother. He was not doing well at all. She went over to his room. He was asleep and in full sweat. She touched his forehead, and it was burning up. He was speaking incoherently, asking for their parents, asking for forgiveness. He kept on saying forgive me, forgive me, I need to wash my hands. I am covered with blood. God forgive me. She sat next to him and hugged him and started praying over him. She prayed for healing of his soul and body. She brought some ice water and a towel and began to place ice packs over his head. His temperature needed to come down. He needed medical attention. She was completely helpless. She was hardly able to walk. Her right ankle continued to swell and hurt. There were no phones. She could only pray and ask the Lord for help. She brought out her bible and read to Philiep. She chose Psalm 91

"Whoever dwells in the shelter of the Most High will rest in the shadow of the Almighty. I will say of the Lord, "He is my refuge and my fortress, my God, in whom I trust." Surely, he will save you from the fowler's snare and from the deadly pestilence. He will cover you with his feathers, and under his wings you will find refuge; his faithfulness will be your shield and rampart. You will not fear the terror of night, nor the arrow that flies by day, nor the pestilence that stalks in the darkness, nor the plague that destroys at midday. A thousand may fall at your side, ten thousand at your right hand, but it will not come near you. You will only observe with your eyes and see the punishment of the wicked......"

She finished reading the Psalm and looked down at her brother. His features had become more relaxed. There was a peaceful look on his face. His color had become more normalized, and his breathing became easy. In a few minutes, he started to snore. He was sleeping restfully. She kept on putting ice packs on his forehead throughout the night catching a few minutes of sleep here and there till she finally fell asleep only to wake up by the terrible noise of a rocket hitting a building close to theirs. Philiep looked much better now. She looked at his wound dressing and there was less drainage. The redness around his wound was much less and the swelling and tenderness were almost gone. She lifted her head up and thanked Jesus. She asked Philiep if he was hungry, when he answered in the positive, she went to the kitchen and prepared some tea, cheese and olives. She brought some bread which was several days old and stale with some fungus on the surface. She cleaned off the fungus as much as she could then brought the breakfast on a tray and sat down beside her brother, and they ate. She turned on the tape recorder to some Fairouz songs. The batteries were still good and she was grateful for that.

One of the songs was about "Mother with Child" referring to Mary and Jesus. She immediately remembered her great aunt Rose. They called her Umm George. How she always loved this song.

She felt warmth and happiness come over her when she remembered her great Aunt. She remembered all the good times she spent with her in the village. She remembered the night times when they would light a fire and roast ears of corn and potatoes. How Rose would read from the Bible to her and then they would share their experiences and thoughts together. They would stay up beyond midnight talking and looking at the stars, listening to the sounds of night. These were such special times. She also remembered George who was Philiep's age. How he was so mercilessly killed without cause, and how brave and forgiving her great Aunt was. She was such a tremendous source of wisdom and encouragement for Layla. She taught her so much, not just by what she told her, but by how she lived her life and how she reacted to people and events. She always reacted with such grace and elegance. She was patient, loving, kind. She does not recall that she ever heard her raise her voice at anyone for any reason. How she loved and missed her now that she was gone from this world, and she can no longer seek her wisdom. She remembered what Rose told her when she asked her about the murderer of her son and whether she wished him dead too? Rose told her: How could I hate the man who killed my son when God's spirit lives in my heart. Believe me I tried to hate him, but I couldn't. Something within me urged me to forgive him. I remained at peace despite my pain. I could see my George dead before my eyes, but I knew that he was alive. Not his body, his true self. His spirit and soul. He knew Christ and believed that all his sins were washed by the blood that was shed on the cross. He had assurance of eternal life and lived his life that way. He was always ready to meet his creator. He called heaven his permanent home and now he is there after finishing his journey. He is not coming back to me, but I am going to him. I will sit with him at the feet of our savior forever. How can I be sad Layla when all that is waiting for me?

Layla didn't know how to answer her back then, but now she knows exactly what Rose was saying. She repeated the words of the apostle Paul: To me life is Christ, and to die is gain.

Chapter 19

Layla woke up with a start when she heard the loud moan her brother gave out. She went over to him and felt his forehead with the back of her hand. His head seemed to be on fire again. He was shaking violently. She quickly went to the ice box and brought out some ice and placed it in water. She got out a towel and started to dip it in ice and wash her brother's head and face with it. He tried to resist but couldn't. He was delirious and was asking for Layla. She kept on telling him that she was right there with him, but he did not seem to hear her.

She started praying over him again asking for a miracle. She uncovered him and brought some rubbing alcohol and started to rub down his shoulders and chest and abdomen. His wound seemed to have stopped draining. She uncovered the bandages and was immediately taken back by the odor and the horrible looking wound. She knew that there was an abscess and that it needed to be drained, or her brother will not see day light.

She went to their storage closet and got out some rope. She placed towels around her brother's arms and legs and tied him down to the bed. He was very strong, and she needed to have him stay still while she opened and drained the abscess.

She poured some iodine over the wound area then went to the kitchen and lit the stove. She took out their sharpest knife and put the blade over the flame till it turned red hot. She cooled the blade with an alcohol-soaked towel then put the edge of the knife to the top edge of the wound and looked up to heaven and said: Ya Yasou' (Oh Jesus). She pushed the tip of the knife into the wound and her brother screamed in anguish. He tried to move, but she had tied him very securely to the bed. She kept on moving the edge of the knife firmly downwards over the wound ignoring his screams. As she did so, the wound opened and a large amount of puss immediately poured out of the wound. She kept cleaning the wound up till she could see no more puss or necrotic tissue. Her brother had passed out from the pain and was quiet now. She breathed a sigh of relief for him. She wiped her tears with the sleeve of her left arm and continued her work silently. She took out the Iodine bottle and poured out some more Iodine over the wound, then she soaked clean gauze in Iodine and packed his wound. She covered everything with torn pieces of linen that she had boiled earlier for this purpose.

She knew that this would give him some relief, and maybe a few more days. The antibiotics had to be obtained at all costs.

She looked down at her ankle and saw that the swelling was down somewhat. She thought that her brother wouldn't wake up till morning. She took her bracelet again and put it in a cloth draw string bag and tied it around her waist. She reinforced the splint that she had made for her ankle, swallowed several Aspirin tablets and grabbed her mother's cane. She went out the door again and out of the building. She kept close to the walls. She was determined that she will get the antibiotics or die trying. Her brother was going to die without them. Might as well that they die together. She will not let him down this time.

She kept on walking fast and ignoring the pain. She used the cane for support. She passed the spot where she was shot at the first time and kept on going. No one bothered her. She walked north for another half an hour keeping low. She knew the streets of Beirut very well. She had lived most of her adult life here and had many friends. They used to visit each other always. There was no fear and Beirut was alive 24 hours a day back then.

She passed her friend's house. Marlene had disappeared that year. She was later found in the southern section raped and murdered. Her mother died 2 weeks after that. She could not live with the thought of what happened to her daughter, and she took a bottle of sleeping pills and died. It was a tragedy, but the type of tragedy they became used to by now.

She reached Borj Hammoud. She knew exactly where to go. She had been at Walid's house before to buy some supplies. It was almost 11:00 pm and she saw light coming from his window. She went up the half torn down stairway to the second floor and knocked on his apartment's door.

He opened the door and smiled. He was drinking and seemed to be somewhat intoxicated. He said: This is just what I need to finish off a good night. A beautiful girl. Come on in.

Layla did not like the feeling she had. He was not very sober, and she did not trust him. She knew that he was capable of evil things. She had no choice however and went in.

She told him what was needed and showed him the bracelet. His eyes lit up when he saw the bracelet and he told her that he had Ampicillin 500. He had a good supply of it and would be happy to give her the antibiotics and syringes and needles as well as more gauze. He had one condition. The bracelet was more than enough for that, but he was not thinking of money now.

His eyes were all over her. Lust was apparent in his eyes. He told her that she had to pay him more than the bracelet. That he wanted her tonight. Layla was terrified. She knew that she should not have come in but she did not feel that she had a choice. She told him that he should be ashamed of himself. He came towards her, and she pushed him away. He became angry and slapped her then reached for her blouse and tried to tear it off. She quickly moved out of the way as he lunged at her and struck him between his shoulder blades very hard with the cane. He fell, shook his head then turned his head towards her and smiled. It was the ugliest smile she had seen in her entire life. She knew that she was in serious trouble. She looked around for an escape and saw a room with a door partially open. She quickly ran into the room, and he was on her heels. The Arak however had clearly had its effect on him, and he was unstable. She got to the room quickly and closed the door and locked it. He started pounding on the door and yelling: Open the door or I will break it down. She looked around the room and saw that it was filled to the ceiling with supplies. This was his storeroom and he had fortified it well. The door was made of solid wood and had a very wide jamb made from oak. The lock was a dead bolt lock. There was an iron bar that could be placed behind the door and into two brackets on each side of the door. She placed the iron bar in and started looking around for the medicine ignoring his yelling and profanities. She had to find the antibiotics first and foremost. She kept on looking around till she found a box that was filled with ampules of powder. She saw the antibiotics and took 20 small ampules. She wrapped them carefully and tucked them between her breasts. She looked around some more and saw some bottles of alcohol and Iodine and syringes. She took what she needed and looked around for something to hold it in. She found an old canvas bag. She put all that she had in it and took a deep breath. She needed to get out now. All she had to do was wait for him to sleep. With all the Arak that she smelled on his breath, she knew she didn't have to wait long.

She listened carefully through the door. It was less than 15 minutes before she heard him snore. She waited an additional 10 minutes to make sure. When his snoring got heavier, she opened the door slowly and stepped around him then bolted out of the apartment door. Her heart was beating very fast. She was scared, but happy that she got the antibiotics.

She kept on moving fast avoiding all light. She ducked behind the rubble whenever she could. It took her almost one hour to get back home. She opened the door slowly. She did not want to wake Filiep up. She put the bag down and went to his room to check on him. As she entered the room, she immediately froze in her place with a look of terror on her face…

Chapter 20

Fadi and Hazem woke up feeling very sick. Their stomachs were aching and their guts wanted to spit out everything inside. It was a cold night they spent without any shelter or cover. They ached for some hot fluids. They got up and started the motorcycle, but it would not start. They tried again without any luck. Hazem looked at the fuel gauge and it read empty. He lifted his head up and thanked God. He got them to where they needed to be. They will walk the rest of the distance into the camp.

The sun was out now and slowly starting to warm up the day. They felt much better as they started to walk. Near the edge of the camp, they were greeted by several blockades with armed men guarding them. One of the men called Nasser knew Fadi and escorted him in. On the way into the camp, he told Nasser of his mission. Nasser knew who Alia was and knew her parents. He took them there in a pickup truck. They got down before a small shack put together from different pieces of tin and plywood and a few cement blocks. The inside of the shack was surprisingly clean and warm. There were several rugs thrown on the ground and covering the walls. There was a table and several chairs to the right of the doorway. In the side opposite the door there was a large sofa and next to it 2 makeshift beds. A narrow corridor led to a smaller area where there was a stove and a small cabinet for food storage. There was also a place to wash up.

Abu Alia came to the door and greeted them and asked them inside. He quickly asked Alia his daughter to make some tea and put some breakfast on the table. Hazem and Fadi felt a rush of joy inside when they heard about tea and breakfast. They were cold and starving.

They told Abu Alia the story and how they found the dying man whose name they never even got. They took out the money, letter and pictures and gave them to the old man. His eyes were wet, but he did not cry. He had known too much pain and misery to cry over a dead loved one anymore. He already lost all that he had ever known in 1948 when the Jews came in. He lost his wife that first year after the diaspora. He lost his mother and sister 5 years later to hunger and disease. And since the war, he lost his two sons.

He took the package from Fadi and thanked him for bringing it to his daughter. He asked Fadi not to mention anything to her right now. He wanted to tell her himself when they were alone together later.

Alia brought in breakfast and hot tea. They broke bread together and ate at the table all four of them. Many times, during breakfast Fadi found it very hard to swallow his food whenever he thought of what this very lovely young woman was going to go through when she found out that her husband is no more.

They finished breakfast and sat down for a while longer sipping tea. News had spread through the camp of their arrival and many visitors came to the old man's shack to ask of news of what was happening north of the camps. Fadi and Hazem told them that the situation is only getting worse. The presence of Syrian troops may have halted some of the violence of Lebanese against Lebanese but brought on a new form of destruction. The Syrians had tanks and heavy guns and bombarded different sites in Lebanon daily. No one was happy with the way things were going. The Palestinians knew very well that the presence of Syrian troops in the territory will be an excuse for Israel to use for further incursions into South Lebanon and further displacement of Palestinian refugees.

The men in the shack started to argue over the political situation. They started to talk about the impending doom. They have had plenty of experience with how politics worked in the Middle East so that they could predict the upcoming events very well. They knew what was to come. They were preparing for an Israeli incursion already. They were mostly upset at Saad Haddad and his SLA. They did not like the fact that a group of Lebanese were aiding Israel against the Palestinians. They knew however that in a way, it was some of the Palestinian elements that caused this to happen. They should not have attacked the very same people who gave them refuge. Lebanon was not their country, yet they acted as if South Lebanon had always belonged to them. They lost Palestine and wanted to form a new homeland. Only the Lebanese weren't willing to give up a part of their country to the Palestinians.

The situation was very complicated. Many factors were thrown in the mix. There were many ethnic sects in Lebanon each with a different political agenda. There were the Lebanese Mauranite Christian majority. There were the Armenians, The Assyrians, The Druz, The Sunni Moslems, The Shi'ite Moslems, The Palestinian refugees and many smaller ethnicities. There were many religious parties as well, some were moderate, but most were extremists that did not except anyone else's views. There were Lebanese Nationalists, Pro-Syrian Pan Arab Nationalists, George Habash and his Marxist faction, Communists, Separatists and Anarchists.

There were also many countries involved in the conflict. Israel and Syria were the major players. Israel was backed by the United States of America and Syria backed by the Soviet Union. The Middle East had always been a battle ground where these two superpowers played out their differences. France was historically entwined with Lebanon. Many nations saw that instability in Lebanon may lead to instability in the entire Middle East and another war involving Israel with its Arab neighbors, a war that may drag with it the Super-powers.

Cigarette smoke, the small enclosure and the number of people present made it very stuffy inside the shack. Fadi and Hazem needed to get out for a while and walk around. They did not feel in any way threatened. They walked around the camp between the shacks and tents. There were very few homes built from cement blocks or bricks. It was a run-down camp with garbage and refuse everywhere. Junk from old cars, motorcycles, rusty pipes, pieces of wood and tin were a common site. A piece from an airplane wing was seen behind one of the shacks. There was lots of mud everywhere. The streets between the enclosures were not organized. They twisted around like snakes. Some were wider than others. Some antennas could be seen over the larger shacks. Radios were already blasting with Arabic music. The aroma of onions and garlic being sautéed filled the space around them. They saw children everywhere. Most were half naked, most were bare foot. They seemed dirty. Their clothes were torn and old. Fadi and Hazem saw misery and hunger everywhere they looked. Strangely enough, people in the camps did not seem as disturbed by these sites as they were. Fadi said: I suppose that people can adapt to just about anything. Humans are so resilient. Look Hazem, these children are playing and laughing and having a good time as if they were in the middle of a classy neighborhood in Beirut.

Hazem said: Mankind is always looking for ways to make their lives more comfortable, but when it comes down to it we can survive with very little. Look at how happy we were today just to be inside a warm home and eat a simple meal. I don't think that I would have been any happier had I been in the Miranda in Beirut.

Fadi laughed and they continued to walk for a while more then they went back to Abu Alia's shack. When they got there, it seemed that all was normal. There were still a few men talking and smoking. Apparently, Alia had not heard the news yet.

They told Nasser that they had to leave and asked if he could give them a ride back to the motorcycle and provide them with some gasoline. Nasser told them to wait around for another day. He said that he lives alone in his shack and would be happy to have them spend the night there. He also told them that Abu Nidal, one of the leaders in the camp invited them to lunch. He even slaughtered a chicken for the occasion and will be very offended if you refuse.

Hazem and Fadi were very grateful. They knew the great need in this camp. A chicken may not sound like much, but when it's all you have and you offer it to strangers, it means much. Arabs were always so hospitable.

Fadi and Hazem accepted the invitation and went with Nasser towards one of the larger homes in the camp. A guard with a Kalashnikov was standing by the door. Inside they heard the sounds of talk and arguments. The smell of smoke could be detected from the outside. Another typical Arab home. They went inside and said: Salam Alaikum......

Chapter 21

Layla could not move at all. She could not scream or speak. Her brother was lying down on the floor blood pouring from a fresh wound on the side of his head. His ear was partially cut off. He must have been hit very hard with an object. Next to him stood a man with a knife held in his hands. He was pointing the knife at Feliep and yelling at him: You miserable dog! Did you think you were going to escape me? You killed my younger brother and my sister. I will make sure you die slowly and painfully. I will cut you into small pieces. I will start with your ears and then your fingers, I will slice them one by one. I will then cut out your stomach and take out your intestines while you watch. Your last hours in life are going to be very painful. You will pay for what you have done.

He was so wrapped up in what he was saying and doing that he didn't hear Layla come in. Filiep was almost unconscious. He felt Layla come in as he sensed the sudden change in temperature and the faint breeze coming from the direction of the door, but did not look towards her or stir. He was praying that she would leave him alone and escape with her life.

Layla slowly gathered her wits and composure. She moved swiftly to her left and away from the door. She was now directly in the back of the intruder. She slowly picked up the heavy bronze statue of St. George killing the Dragon and held it firmly in both hands. The man now started to slice her brother's ear off. As Filiep screamed in anguish and pain, the man started laughing. Only his laugh did not last long. A loud thump was heard, and he grunted and fell sideways, knife falling from his hand as he lay still next to her brother.

She quickly rushed to Filiep and helped him up to the sofa. She tore the apiece off the pillow case and wrapped it tightly around his head and ear. She needed to stop the bleeding immediately. He had no more blood to lose. He was very weak as it is. He looked half dead as she was tending to him. He tried to point to the man, and she immediately understood what he wanted. She went quickly to the storage closet and got out the rope that she used earlier on her brother and tied the man's hands and feet behind his back. His head was bleeding, but she did not care at that point. He brought this unto himself. Her priority now was to take care of her own brother, then she would see to him.

She heated some water, then washed her brother's face and scalp with it. She brought out the Iodine and cleansed his wounds. She didn't know what to do with his half-torn ear. She simply bound it tightly with bandages after sprinkling some Penicillin powder over the wound. She then boiled the syringe and needle then let it cool a bit. She filled an ampule of Ampicillin with some sterile water then drew the mixture in the syringe. She tapped it a few times till the mixture became milky white and smooth. She injected the antibiotics in her brother's left buttock. She gave him another injection of morphine which she had just brought back with her. He seemed to feel much better after the morphine injection, and he went back to sleep.

She did not have time to panic. She had to do something with this man. He attempted to torture and kill her brother, yet she felt no hate towards him. She understood the pain he was going through. She knew that revenge would not have made him feel any better. He did not know that yet. She started to wipe his scalp with a towel wet with warm water. The gash in his skull was deep. She placed pressure on his scalp for almost 10 minutes till the bleeding stopped completely. She poured some Penicillin powder over the wound and dressed it. He remained unconscious throughout this procedure. She left him tied up on the ground but placed a pillow under his head after turning him on his right side. She did not dare leave him alone in the room with her brother. She was afraid he might wake up and get out of the ropes and kill them both. She slept on the big chair in the corner of the room outside the circle of light that came through the window. She held on to a kitchen knife. She was completely exhausted. She had to fight off a rapist and a murderer in one night. She thanked God for keeping her safe and for bringing her back in time to save her brother.

She went into a light sleep and did not stir but occasionally. Neither the tied-up man nor her brother made a sound. It was five o'clock in the morning when Filiep started to wake up. She immediately was by his side. His head was aching, and he was in terrible pain, but he told her that he felt much better. By opening his festered wound she saved his life, he told her. Her hand was on his forehead feeling his temperature and he kissed her hand. He looked very fondly at her and said: Thank you my angel. She smiled and kissed his forehead.

Fileip then looked down at the man that was bundled up and said: Is he dead?

-I don't know. I hit him very hard with St. George. He has not stirred since last night.

-Why don't you put some water on his face and see if that wakes him up.

She went to the kitchen and brought a pitcher of water with her. She slowly poured the water over the man's face. He woke up with a startle and coughed heavily. He could barely raise his head up. He kept his eyes closed. It was very apparent that the light made his headache all the more severe.

-What's your name, and why did you want to kill me so badly?

-Name is Omar Hamadeh. You killed my younger brother and sister. You brought down the building on their heads along with 20 other people. You are a monster, and you deserve to die.

-A monster I am, and deserve to die, I do. But it is not my time yet. And I am not going to be killed by you.

-If I don't kill you, somebody else will. You brought a lot of sorrow to many people.

-And I suppose that you are innocent. That your hands are clean of our blood. What you tried to do to me yesterday could only be done by an animal. What should we do with you now? We can't let you go; you will be back to kill me again. I must kill you.

Layla said immediately and in a very stern voice that brought both men to attention: No more killing! Are you both still hungry for blood. How many people do you want to kill before you are satisfied? You love killing so much, look at you. You are worse than animals. She put her hands over her face and ran to the kitchen crying.

Filiep said: Look now what you have done to my sister. I should punish you just for that alone.

-Go ahead and kill me if you wish. I no longer care to live. Life has no meaning any longer. Life is worse than shit.

-I don't blame you for wanting to kill me. I have to tell you that I had never killed or hated anyone before the war. It was all the friends I lost that were killed by you people that turned me into a killer. I suppose the same happened to you.

-I was a music teacher. I never harmed anyone in my entire life. After my brother and sister died, I lost my mind. I wanted to kill every Mourani in site. Some friends of mine found out that it was you who bombed our building. It took me two years to finally catch up with you. I wanted to do every horrible thing I could imagine to you before killing you.

-You may not have to worry about me much longer anyway. The way I look and feel, I may not last long at all. Look, I understand your grief and despite you cutting half of my ear off, I will not harm you.

I just need to make sure that you will never try to harm us again. I can't take a chance on letting you go. That is my dilemma. I truly don't know what to do with you.

The man looked down and whimpered: I should not have failed. I should have taken revenge for my sister and brother. You were so helpless before me and I almost had you. I don't know where your sister came from, but like you said, it was not your day to die.

Layla came into the room with the knife in her hand and approached the man. She crouched next to him, and he looked at the knife then at her eyes. He expected to see murder in her eyes instead, he saw tears.

She said: No one is going to die today if I can help it. She sliced the ropes from his hands and feet and set him free. She told him to leave and not come back. She said: My brother has paid dearly for the atrocities he committed and is still paying. He may or may not live due to his wounds. I will do everything in my power to help him live. I want him to live so that he does not go to his grave with all that blood on his hands. I want him to atone for what he did and to seek forgiveness from God. I advise you to do the same. If you love your sister, listen to me. She would not have wanted you to become a bloody monster.

The man put his head between his knees and his hands over his head and started to sob. He continued to do so for several minutes then he slowly got up and headed towards the door. He stopped just short of the door and looked at Layla and said: Thank you sister. Fadwa looked just like you. I promise you before God that I will never attempt to harm you or your brother again. May God forgive both of us for all that we have done. Then he left quietly.

Chapter 22

Fadi and Hazem were drinking tea with Abu Nidal and his men. They had an excellent lunch. This was the first time Hazem had Maftoul. Fadi had it a few times before when he visited the camps with Layla. Maftoul was a popular Palestinian dish made from pasta that was rolled into tiny balls and cooked with chicken, carrots and chickpeas. They ate it with rice and had radishes and green onions on the side. Fadi and Hazem have not had such a meal for a long time. The men as always started discussing politics. Abu Nidal said that some of his spies saw some large troop aggregations just north of Beit Jann and northeast of Hurfeish. More troops seemed to be headed west from Qiryat Shemona. He was told that several tank divisions were already on the move north.

Fadi and Hazem had been listening all day long to this kind of talk. The prevailing opinion was that Israel was preparing for an attack. Fadi told Hazem that if Israel attacked Southern Lebanon, there would be blood to the knees. The situation was just too explosive and there were many factions. The whole area was like a keg of powder ready to explode.

Fahd and Hazem thanked Abu Nidal for his hospitality and excused themselves. They went with Nasser to his shack and took a small nap. When they woke up, Nasser had some tea ready. They sat down on straw chairs and started to talk while sipping tea.

Nasser asked Fadi about the situation in the Beqaa valley. He asked if the Syrians were in complete control of the sector, and if he approved of their presence in Lebanon.

Fadi said: I don't approve of this entire war anymore. You know what kind of soldier I am. Lately however I have changed. I don't want to see any more bloodshed. I don't understand why peace can't be negotiated.

Nasser said: You can't negotiate with the devil. If you give Israelis a fingernail, they will take your whole arm with it. They don't want peace with us. They want to exterminate us.

-I don't believe that all Israelis are bad. Look, many of them are already fighting their own government for Palestinian rights. They too want to be able to live peacefully and see their children grow and get married and bring them grandchildren. The aspirations of all people are the same. There is not that much difference. When you come to think of it, Jews and Arabs are cousins.

Nasser laughed and said: I am not surprised. We got too many of the same traits. Where in the world can you find more religious zealots and stubborn people than among Arabs and Jews? What's funnier is that Ismael and Isaac are brothers. Both are sons of Abraham.

Hazem interjected: Then why are the sons of Abraham trying to kill each-other?

Fadi commented: It is funny that Christians, Moslems and Jews claim Abraham as their father, yet throughout history they continuously slaughtered each other.

Hazem said: Had Sarah not convinced Abraham to use Hager to bear him a son, all this would not have happened. Sarah then expels Hager and Ishmael, making matters worse. You see, when you get down to it, all troubles in this world are caused by women.

All three of them laughed. How typical it is of Arab men to blame everything on women, Fadi said as they continued to laugh.

Their laughter was cut short however by the sound of shelling and machine guns. The skyline to the south of the camp became dark gray. Dust and gun fire smoke obliterated the southern horizon. The sounds were becoming closer with every passing minute.

The camp suddenly became like a busy beehive. Young men appeared from every direction carrying all sorts of weapons. Several pick-ups came out of nowhere. They had machine guns mounted on them. They headed south out of the camp.

Nasser went into his shack and came out with an SG 540 assault rifle and several round belts. He told Fadi and Hazem that it was time to defend our land. They took it from us once, they are not going to take it again.

A jeep drove quickly by and Nasser jumped into it. Fadi and Hazem stood there not sure what to do. As Nasser continued looking at them along with the jeep driver, they jumped into the jeep as well. The jeep took off immediately and zigzagged through the different dwellings. As they neared the southern edge of the camp, an explosion less than 30 meters away rocked their jeep. Other explosions nearby were heard. Tanks now could be heard in the distance as if they were roaring thunder. The sky darkened with smoke and shells started to land everywhere. There were at least 50 different types of trucks and jeeps and smaller vehicles that came out of the camp and went south to face the tanks. Other men were running behind the vehicles with grenade launchers and shoulder held anti-tank rocket launchers. They took positions into pre-dug trenches. Other men now started pouring out of the camp from all directions and taking up defensive positions. Shells rained mercilessly into the camp. One shack after another fell into rubble as the shells exploded. Fire and smoke filled the camp along with screams of anguish as occupants ran blindly between the shacks, some of them on fire. Others were half burned walking blindly asking for help. One boy less than 10 years of age was running out of the camp with his left arm barely hanging to his body. His face was blackened and clothes bloodied and torn. Fadi jumped out of the jeep and ran towards him. He picked him up in his arms and ran back into the camp. He went into the first shack he saw. There was an old man and his wife who was not much younger than he was. They were both cowering in the corner. There was a small bed. He put the boy on it and asked the woman to get him some linen. She just looked at him in shock and did not move or utter a word. Her eyes were looking past him and onto a picture of her son that was hung on the tin wall over the bed. He looked around quickly and saw an old shirt. There was no mending of the arm now. His main goal was to stop the bleeding. He tied the shirt around the boy's arm and tightened it as much as possible. The boy screamed in pain. He was still bleeding. He took a spoon that was nearby and slipped it into the knot and began to twist it till the bleeding stopped. He tied the spoon down to keep the pressure on the arm. He did not notice that the boy had already passed out till now. He could hear more explosions and screams all around him. He left the boy with the old man and woman and went out. He saw a woman running out of her shelter with her rope burning. She was frantic and trying to put out the fire. She was screaming hysterically and running in all directions. He ran quickly to her. He reached for her rope and pulled it off of her. He could smell the hair on his arms burn and then felt the sting of pain as the fire seared his arms. He ignored his pain and quickly took off his shirt and covered the woman's bare upper body. He let her fall to the ground and ran further into the camp then stood there for a minute. There was complete chaos everywhere. Rubble and fire throughout the camp. Dead and dying people. Body parts. Ongoing explosions. People running around like chickens with their heads cut off. It was a horrible site. He knew he was brought here by God to help these people. He just felt completely overwhelmed and useless.

He shook away his fear and shock. He needed to help these people at all costs. This was his Jihad now. He crossed himself for the first time in his life then ran into the fray.

Chapter 23

Maj. Gilad gave the orders to move. The incursion into Lebanon had been approved. His aid immediately got on the phone and repeated the orders. Within minutes, the sounds of tank engines filled the air. Troops began to assemble. Jeeps began to move. Heavy artillery was attached to the wagons and army trucks stood in line as thousands of soldiers poured out of their tents with their full combat dress on. This was precision in mass. Every single soldier knew what was expected of him and knew which role he played. It took less than 30 minutes for all troops to be ready, the slow march towards the North then began. The objective was to drive all PLO and Shi'ite fighters out of Southern Lebanon and North of the Litani River.

As Major Gilad's division moved northward, so did other divisions that were close to the border. This was a well-planned and coordinated incursion. The events of the last few days with the massacre in Tel Aviv contributed in part to the timeline only. This event, however, was not planned in haste or as a reaction to these events.

Daoud was riding in the back seat of his Jeep. His driver was Turai (Private) Amir. Amir was only 19 years old; he knew. He asked him if this was his first combat mission. Amir answered that it was.

-Are you scared Amir.

-A bit Sir. Although I am ready to serve my country. I believe in our cause.

-Which cause is that Amir?

-Defending Israel against all enemies and preserving our boundaries Sir.

-I too believe in defending Israel against all enemies. I am just not sure that we can call helpless refugees enemies.

-Our enemies are not helpless Sir. They have plenty of weapons. They keep raiding our northern towns and causing trouble. They hide in the refugee camps among civilians so that we can't bomb them. I deplore their tactics. How many of our people have they killed?

-I agree with you on that point Amir. Their tactics are deplorable. Suicide bombings and airplane hijackings and kidnappings. I am sick of that myself. What troubles me however is the fact that we are going in there now knowing fully well that this incursion will cause significant collateral damage. We will in fact be killing hundreds of innocent civilians and displacing thousands of people from their meager homes yet once more. I can't bring myself to agree with that.

-Yes Sir. I understand what you are saying Sir. Frankly, that troubles me too. I am no child killer. Some of my comrades justify killing Palestinian children by saying that when they grow up they will become PLO fighters and kill us. So, if we kill them now, we can prevent them from killing our people in the future.

-That is a sick logic. What have we turned into? Look, I believe in our state. I believe that we needed a national home for Jews to come to. Jews have been persecuted throughout the centuries everywhere. We have been beaten, ridiculed, spat at and killed. What happened to us in Germany and Eastern Europe is not new. It had happened to us on a smaller scale throughout history starting with our exile to Babylon. What troubles me is the way we did it. We did not buy lands or take lands that were not occupied. Instead, we displaced hundreds of thousands of people and took away their homes and lands by force. This is how our statehood was established. God gave this land to

Abraham and his descendants. Yet according to the profits, it was his will to exile us to Babylon. In addition, he told us not to rebel against other nations or go back in mass to Israel until our Messiah comes. He warned us of travesty if we did not obey. Look at what has been happening to our people since we occupied this land. We have not seen any kind of peace since then. You are 19 years old and here you are. Instead of studying in college now, you are on your way to a battle where you have to kill or possibly be killed. Somehow, I can't justify that.

-But Sir, it is our duty, all of us, to defend our nation.

-Yes Amir. I know. I am defending our nation the best way I know how without participating in killing. I am a builder. I will build bridges, homes, hospitals and schools wherever I can. That is where I place all my energies. I am helping to build our nation. That is how I can make it stronger. Killing refugees is not something that I am willing to do, however.

-What if you were in a situation where someone was going to kill you. Will you not kill that person then?

-If I had to defend my life, then yes. But under no other circumstances will I kill another human being. We were all created in God's image. How can we say that we love God and then hate those who were created in his image? It makes no sense to me. This is why I don't carry an assault weapon. Don't need one. I only carry a side arm for self-defense only.

-That makes you a pacifist then Sir.

-No Amir, that makes me a good Jew. We Jews brought the Law of Moses to the world. God chose us to be his people. He wanted us to be a holy nation and live according to his laws. Well, we all know how that went. That is why we became scattered all over the world. It was our sins that separated us from our God. Now, I wonder if we are not rebelling against him yet one more time.

-I have not given God much thought Sir. Our family is not a religious family, but we are Zionists. We believe strongly in the nation of Israel. A nation where every Jew from around the world can come for refuge. This nation Sir must succeed and must be strong.

-My only argument against that Amir, is that we are building our nation by mixing its mortar with the blood of innocents.

As they were talking an order was given to all vehicles to halt. Their first objective was less than 10 Kilometers away. They were ordered to clean out the Nabatieh camp. Intelligence reports linked the camp to many of the attacks into Northern Israel the last year. They needed to drive all anti-Israeli sympathizers out of South Lebanon permanently.

So far there has been minimal resistance. They had a few skirmishes on the way without any major engagements or losses. Few Shi'ite militia men and few PLO sympathizers shelled the moving columns with RPJ rounds and machine guns. One of the tanks was disabled by a shoulder held anti-tank gun. The fighters were promptly dealt with. Their resistance efforts were minute so far. The advancing Israelis were not slowed down by these attacks.

Slowly the outskirts of Nabatyia came into view. This was going to be a little harder now. They knew that they had a hard task ahead of them here. The soldiers knew that they would have to shoot woman and children in the process of cleaning out the camps. Many of the soldiers did not seem to mind. They thought of Palestinians as pests, no more or less. Few of the soldiers however had a very hard time with the idea of shooting civilians. Army psychiatrists played an important role in preparing these soldiers for war and in dealing with the after-effects of it.

Daoud was busy looking at the beautiful landscape as they advanced. He prayed to God for a miracle that will stop this war. He prayed for the peace of Israel and its neighbors daily. He did not hate Arabs.

He had hoped that someday Arabs and Israelis could become good neighbors.

They stopped again and orders were given for the heavy field guns to be positioned. The shelling then started. The entire land scape before them erupted suddenly with explosions. Dirt and smoke rose into the air several meters high. Huge tongues of fire could be seen from among the smoke trying to escape its grip.

After two hours of shelling, the heavy guns stopped, and the tanks started to advance. Behind the tanks were thousands of soldiers and manned vehicles advancing as well.

Resistance was much harder here. The enemy had apparently been prepared and well dug into their trenches. They returned heavy fire. RPJs and heavy machine guns did not do major damage to the advancing wall of tanks but caused several army vehicles to burst into flames and sharp shooters were able to find some soft targets.

Suddenly, Phantoms roared in the sky above like screaming eagles and shook their wings as they flew over the Israelis. It was less than a minute that passed before they let their loads fall over the different defensive positions of the PLO. A wall of fire rose from the ground, and the Phantoms came back for a second pass. They let their load fall again and the ground before Daoud seemed to turn into a lake of fire. The tanks then advanced again and drove over the trenches and over the bodies of the dead, and sometimes, the living. Screams of pain and horror could be heard everywhere. Blood, smoke and fire was all that Daoud could see as his Jeep got closer to the camp now. He saw bodies that were disemboweled and others that were burned. He saw limbs and parts of human bodies spread all over the terrain. He was horrified. He did not want to look anymore.

They entered the main camp now. The picture here was no better than what he saw before. Only, he started to see bodies of women and children now.

Tanks swept over the shanty homes and crushed them to the ground. People were fleeing everywhere. They were frantic. Once in a while a man with a weapon would emerge and would be shot down immediately.

Daoud then saw two men carrying a woman out of a fallen shack. They took her further north into the camp to a larger dwelling that had a white shirt, serving as a white flag, posted on it. The two men came back and carried another woman that was shot in the stomach and leg. He saw them lift their hands up as a soldier lifted his assault rifle to shoot them down. They had no weapons on their bodies. They pointed to the wounded then to the dwelling with the white flag. The soldier laughed at them. He turned to another soldier on his left and said something and they both laughed. He lowered his gun and signaled to them to go ahead.

As the Jeep continued to advance behind the main force, Daoud could not believe his eyes. The amount of destruction and the number of dead was astonishing. He thought that he must have seen at least four to five hundred dead so far.

He looked back once or twice to see if the building with the white flag was still standing. He saw that the building was spared. He was very happy to see that. There was at least a chance that the wounded may be cared for and survive. They had a mobile army medical unit with very capable personnel. He knew that they would not deprive the wounded of care. Most likely they will leave a few soldiers to guard the place and one or two medics to deliver care. He thought of the two men that were carrying the wounded to the house. He admired their bravery and conviction. They had placed their lives on the line to help the wounded. They could have escaped. They took a very bad risk by staying behind. They could have easily been shot down without hesitation by any of the soldiers. He thought that there must have been some divine protection there for these two men….

Chapter 24

Fadi and Hazem ran from one place to another aiding those who were injured. Shells fell all around them. Destruction was massive and was everywhere. Cries of anguish were heard from every direction. A woman ran past them half naked and screaming calling out for her son. She was bare foot. Her hair was half burned off and an ugly gash was on the back of her neck. Others were running in all directions. There was total confusion in the camp. They had to act quickly. They could not leave the wounded behind and run. They had to help. This is why God brought them here.

Fadi said: The main units will be here soon. Abu Nidal's men will not hold them off for long. We must find a place to take the wounded to and we must mark it as neutral, or we will have no chance of saving anybody or even ourselves.

Hazem agreed. He said that the largest place he saw was Abu Nidal's house. Fadi agreed. They went to Abu Nidal's home and Fadi climbed up to the tin roof. He tied a white shirt to the TV antenna then jumped back down. Then he and Hazem started moving the injured into the house. A young lady named Nabilah saw what they were doing and decided to stay behind and help. She said that she had nursing skills. Fadi told her that she could be killed if she stayed behind and tried to convince her to leave, but she would not listen. He quickly then agreed and thanked God for the help. They started to bring people in till there was no room anymore. One of the men that was helped started to help Nabilah in turn. Soon they had five volunteers helping them.

There were no supplies. They were mainly stopping the bleeding and removing any apparent shrapnel that they could detect. One of the men found a bottle of Arak and some Iodine and cotton. They used Arak and Iodine as an antiseptic whenever they could. Nabilah found some coffee grounds and she started using those to stop any bleeding. One of the men started to heat water to wash wounds with.

Fadi and Hazem went outside looking for wounded people that can still be helped when a Jeep stopped before them and the soldier pointed his assault rifle at them and spoke in Hebrew. They could not understand what he was saying but did not want him to misinterpret the situation. They raised their hands in the air and Fadi pointed to the white flag on Abu Nidal's house then to the wounded in the street. The soldier was amused. He said something to his companion in Hebrew and they both laughed. He then waved them on and drove past them. Another Jeep was behind them. In that Jeep was a driver and another soldier. The soldier surprisingly did not carry any assault rifle or a weapon except for a gun that was holstered to his waste. As the Jeep passed by, they looked at each other and their eyes Locked for a second. Fadi could not see any hate in those eyes. He saw remorse and empathy. The Jeep drove away as he and Hazem carried another injured man to Abu Nidal's house.

They had to find more supplies. Fadi took his white undershirt off and tied it to a stick. He went outside and tried to flag down what he thought might have been a medical car. He knew that he was taking a risk and that he may be shot. He lifted his eyes to heaven and asked God for protection. He had killed many people in his past. This was his opportunity to save lives instead and he was not going to waste it.

The vehicle stopped and someone spoke to him in broken Arabic: What are you doing here? Are you trying to be killed? Why didn't you run like the others?

Fadi answered: I am not a resistance fighter. I was just visiting the camp. I am trying to help the wounded. Please give us some supplies. We have no gauze or antiseptic or anything left except some hot water. We need help.

-Whose we?

-I have my friend who was also visiting with me trying to deliver a package to someone, and we have five volunteers. We just need supplies.

-We can't spare much. The supplies are for our soldiers. I will give you some bottles of Iodine and antibiotic powder and some pads and gauze. Do the best you can with them. I will put in a request to send you some help. We will have two soldiers stay with you and make sure that you don't get into any trouble, and that you cause none yourself!

-Thank you. Blessed are the merciful for they shall obtain mercy.

-I see that you are quoting Yeshua, You are a Christian then? Well, I don't know about mercy here. All I see is blood and gore and destruction. But thank you for the blessing anyway. I can surely use it.

He drove his vehicle away after giving Fadi some medical supplies. Two soldiers stayed at the entrance of the house now. Other soldiers were combing the camp. Once in a while a burst of gun fire could be heard. It was apparent however that the main force had already passed on and was now headed north towards the Litani River.

Fadi went back into Abu Nidal's house, which now became a makeshift field hospital. He distributed the supplies and went back out again looking for more wounded to help.

Chapter 25

Filiep looked at his sister again and thanked her. He told her that he would have been dead a hundred times over by now was it not for her.

She told him how much she loved him. She wanted him to make up for all the wrong that he had done. She told him that he couldn't turn the clock back, and he can't undo the terrible things that he had done. But he can find forgiveness in Jesus and can start a new life. He can't change the past, but he can become free of the guilt that is associated with it. He needed to repent with all his heart and confess his guilt before God. She told him that Christ had already paid the price for his sins on thc cross.

-You can be forgiven. I don't want to see you leave this world with your soul and heart corrupt with hate and your hands stained with blood.

Filiep told her that he wanted to be free of guilt. That he can't sleep one night without having a nightmare about something he had done. He told her that he sees the faces of people he killed haunting him all the time. His physical pain was nothing in comparison to the anguish in his soul. He needed redemption and absolution and didn't believe that he deserved either one.

His injuries were severe. His legs were now numb, and he could no longer feel his middle half. He wasn't sure if he was paralyzed or just very weak. He had an odd sensation; one he had never felt before.

Despite how hot his body was, he felt as if a cold blanket was slowly descending over him. His mind felt as if it was tingling. He laughed at that. How could his mind tingle, but that is what it felt like!

His sister caught his laugh and came closer to him. What is so funny? She spoke.

-It is a weird sensation that I am having. I just think that it is funny.

-Layla laughed and said: whatever it is you're feeling, I am glad it is making you laugh instead of cry. It is better than all the pain you have been having. It could be that the medications are making you feel this way.

-This has nothing to do with the medications. It is something I have never experienced before. I have a premonition that I won't be here for long sis.

-Don't say that. You are going to be alright now that you are taking the antibiotics.

-I don't believe I will. I am worried about you. I want to make sure that you will be Ok if I die.

-Filiep, don't say that. You will not die and leave me alone. Please be strong and survive. For me!

-If I can give you my life sis. I will not hesitate, but this is outside our control. Neither you, nor I, can stop what is to come. I just want to make sure that you are well prepared.

-Don't think about me. Think about getting better only. I want you to pray for that.

-I will pray with you once we talk about our plans. I want you to know what steps to take, where to go, whom to trust and where to get money and food.

Filiep and Layla spoke for a couple of hours after that. She did not want to participate in the conversation, but her brother made her listen. He gave her careful instructions and warned her from staying in Beirut. He told her that she needs to find a way to leave Lebanon and go to America. Their cousin Elias will help her there. She can find work and a new life. The Lebanon she loved has gone forever, he told her.

She objected to what he was saying, but he would not stop. He kept on giving her advice and instructions till he finally felt very weak. He told her then that he wanted to pray with her.

She knelt beside him and caressed his hair, then kissed him on his forehead. He smiled. He felt very peaceful and warm at the touch of her hand. He lifted his head up and strained the musculature around his eyes. His eye lids were burned shut. He spoke out loud:

-Lord God, forgive me. With all my heart I regret the life I lived far from you. My hate and stubbornness caused me to do vile things. I have lived against your will and your laws all my life. I don't deserve your love or your mercy, but I know that you are merciful and that you love me. I repent before you, my God. I am a wretched human being…what's left of me. For the sake of the precious blood that your son shed on the cross for me, I ask your forgiveness and salvation. I ask you to cleanse me from all the evil that I have done. I want to meet you as savior and not as judge. I give you my life, if you choose to give me any more days on this earth. If not, then I entrust my eternity into your hands and I leave Layla in your care. Thank you, Jesus.

Layla was kneeling next to him praying and crying. He finally made his peace with God. He finally received forgiveness. She was crying with joy for her brother's salvation. She looked upon his face and saw peace for the first time in a very long time.

He slowly turned his face to her, and with a smile he said: I can leave now. I love you Layla. Take care of yourself. I leave you in God's hands. His last words trailed slowly from his lips as his head relaxed completely to the side, and his hand fell from Layla's hand…..

Chapter 26

The makeshift hospital was now filled with wounded. Fadi and Hazem had brought in at least fifty people. They were placed everywhere, on the sofas, bed, carpet, floor, and those who could sit sat on the few chairs available or on the floor. Many of the wounded were passed out from loss of blood or from pure agony and pain. Many were badly burned. One man had his arm blown off. The wound was sealed by a bad burn that covered the remaining portion of the arm. Another woman was bleeding from her abdomen, a pool of blood was slowly gathering underneath her garments.

There was also a young girl no more than five years old. Her arm was broken and twisted in a strange fashion. They had tied her arm with a shawl and an older lady was sitting her in her lap. Her hair was reddish-brown and wild. Fragments of what seemed to be burned wood were caught in her hair. Her face was blackened by ashes. Her small red lips and the white of her eyes seemed to be out of place in the landscape of her face. She looked puzzled and scared. Her eyes wandered from one person to another. When her eyes rested on the man with the blown off arm, she shrank then hid her face in the woman's bosom and let out a short cry. The woman slowly tightened her arms around her without saying a single word. She started to rock her slowly back and forth while tears rolled gently down her cheeks.

The volunteers were working frantically. Huda was one of the volunteers who was working on a woman that was shot through the shoulder. She had already stopped the bleeding by using ground coffee compress. She dressed the wound on the shoulder and tied the woman's arm in a sling then moved on to the next person. The other volunteers were as busy.

Once in a while one of the soldiers would peak in and look around. He would soon shake his head in disbelief and go back to his post.

Fadi and Hazem ran back and forth carrying wounded. They were now completely drenched in blood and sweat. They were exhausted and fatigued. They could not stop. There were so many people that needed help. They heard screaming everywhere. The fire, smoke and dust from the attack permeated the camp and most of the dwellings were in rubble.

Several soldiers suddenly showed up in a Jeep. They started speaking in broken Arabic to Fadi when they came close to him. They told him that they were sent by Rav najad Daoud with medical supplies. There were four of them and they appeared to be regular soldiers. Fadi asked if there were any medics among them, they said that there weren't. The medics were needed for the Israeli army. One of them spat next to Fadi and said: If it was up to me, I wouldn't bring you anything.

His mate in the back of the Jeep looked at him with a frown, then shook his head. He didn't say anything. He pulled out four large bags and dumped them over the Jeep next to Fadi. The driver turned the Jeep around quickly sending dust into the air then raced off again to the North.

Chapter 27

The earth in late November was covered with a blanket of snow outside of O'Hare International Airport in Chicago. Layla had been accustomed to snow. The mountains of Lebanon were covered with it for a good portion of the year. She had skied "The Cedars at Mount Makmel", and the slopes at "Farya Mzaar". Elias had met her at the international terminal along with his wife Fayrose. They both hugged and welcomed her heartily. They escorted her with her bags to the parking lot. Elias was driving a gold-colored Cadillac Seville Sedan. He warmed up the car and turned on the heat. Layla was sitting in the back with Fayrose. The heated seats were warm and she felt immediately relaxed. It was night and the snow was still falling. The lights on the highway shone brightly over the falling snowflakes and were reflected off in a mesmerizing fashion. The Christmas decorations were already up on many of the homes. The lights and decorations were joyful and amazing. The different arrays of colored lights were blinking in varying rhythms and styles. Store signs were lit everywhere. The houses seemed quite and serine, hidden among evergreen trees covered with snow. They looked like pictures from the fairy tale books she used to read as a child. Icicles hung from the roofs and branches of trees as tears made of diamonds that slowly elongated and descended gently upon the cheeks of darkness and slumber.

Fayrose was speaking to her, but she could not discern the words. She did not answer. She felt herself a sweet dream, one that she wanted to last. She was very tired from the plane trip, and she felt herself slip slowly into blissful sleep. She awakened briefly once or twice when she felt the car slow down and leave the Highway. There were many streetlights and cars now and she could no longer maintain her slumber. The car was going into smaller streets now and she saw buildings and houses next to each other. None of the buildings were high. Most were two or three stories only. They looked very different from the buildings in Beirut. These were mostly made from brick and wood or other materials that looked like plastic to her. She laughed. How could these buildings withstand the rain and snow and wind? Even a stone thrown by a child could do some damage to these walls, she thought.

She was finally in America. Was she ever to see Lebanon again? Now that Filiepe was dead and many of her relatives have left Lebanon and went off to Canada and France and South America, and some to the United States of America. It seemed that Lebanon became deserted. Even her village was now mostly destroyed due to the frequent shelling by the Syrian artillery.

Her tears started to swell up when she remembered Aunt Rose and her grandparents' house. The fig and walnut groves where she used to play hide and seek with the other girls in the village, and sometimes with Fadi. She remembered evening time when all the cows and sheep would come back from pasture. How they would trot in the narrow cobblestone streets. She remembered the sounds the hoofs made on the stone, along with the sounds of lowing and bleating and bells ringing. How they would be led to the different homes. She couldn't understand how every owner got back all his livestock every evening. How they would not be mixed up with other livestock. How everything seemed to be in such disarray, yet everything ended in a desired outcome. This truly was a situation of controlled chaos. She knew this was an oxymoron but couldn't think of a better description.

The car turned into a driveway of a small house and the garage door opened. Layla stepped out of the car and followed Fayrose into the house while Elias brought in the luggage.

The house was small and warm. It was a two-story home. Through the garage she came into a kitchen which was connected to a dining room with a simple table and 4 chairs. The living room was two steps below the dining area. There was a fireplace in it and Layla could see that some ambers were still glowing. The bedrooms were upstairs. Fayrose showed her the room in which she would stay. It was a small room but was furnished very nicely. New bedcovers were on the bed, and they matched the curtains hung on the windows. There was a dresser and a mirror in the room and two-night tables with lamps. There was also a small closet in the room. Some pictures of Lebanon were hung on the walls.

Layla took her coat and boots off then collapsed over the bed. She was extremely tired and sleepy. Elias and Fayrose were good enough to leave her alone to rest. She put her head on the pillow and drifted quickly into a deep sleep. She had many dreams that night. Dreams of childhood, her village in Lebanon which somehow was here in America. Images of war were overwhelmingly present in her dreams. There were also other images of her brother and their home in Beirut, and there were dreams of her and Fadi walking together in a snowy forest…

Chapter 28

The battle of Southern Lebanon continued for several days. Israeli troops crossed the Litani River and were pushing further north. Several thousand Palestinian and Lebanese civilians were killed during the operation. In addition, close to 200,000 were displaced. Most were Shi'ite Moslems. PLO fighters fled to the North and continued to mount surprise attacks. Abu Nidal and his men rejected any offer of a cease fire. Despite UN resolutions calling for complete withdrawal of all Israeli forces from Southern Lebanon and an immediate end to the aggression, both sides continued to fight for several more days till a settlement was finally established. Most of those who were in camp Nabatieh moved further north and west to Ein El-Hilwe camp.

Hazem and Fadi along with other volunteers helped save Hundreds of wounded. After the Red Cross arrived in the area Fadi and Hazem continued to help for several more days. When they felt that their help was no longer needed, they headed north and into central Lebanon again. Fadi had told Hazem that he intended to go into Beirut and look for Layla.

He wanted to see her badly. All this death around him made his soul yearn for the sight of her. For the sound of her voice and the touch of her hand. The smell of her hair. The look in her eyes when she wanted to tease him. He longed so much for her. She was the only sane thing in his life right now. Because of her, he continued to regard life as a beautiful gift. Because of her, he wanted to live. And because of her, he wanted to redeem himself. He wanted to be worthy of her love.

His faith in Jesus made him a new man. He continued to read the Bible daily. He was amazed at the sense of peace and joy he derived from reading the word of God. Sometimes he would raise his eyes to the sky and start praising God for all his goodness, his eyes would tear up and his being would be flooded with an overwhelming gladness.

He heard others blame and curse God for what was happening to them. They blamed God for the terrible war and all its atrocities. He could not see why God was to blame. If God tells us not to kill, then we go and kill, then how can we blame him for the consequences of our actions. How can we say: Well, why did he allow it to happen? Isn't he in control and can do anything?

Fadi would think about these questions at times and wonder at the hardness of people's hearts. Their blasphemous words even during these terrible times of crisis when they needed to be praying for God's intervention instead. But such was human nature, Fadi thought. We mankind don't easily accept blame. It is easier to blame God, destiny or luck, or other people for what had events go on in our lives. The events that occur in our lives are an outcome of our own actions. It is a matter of law. Physical law demands that for every action there is an equal and opposite reaction. In moral law transgressions require a punishment equal to the degree of transgression. In natural law choices have consequences that drive the progression of our lives. When God created man, he decided to give him free choice. He did not imprison or enslave him. This freedom of choice is the most precious gift to mankind and one that carries the most awesome of responsibilities. This is why people throughout history cherished freedom above all other values including their own lives. To live free or die is a cry heard in all parts of the world throughout history and one that was a preclude to events that often changed the course of history. But this freedom is precisely why God's interventions in our lives are not so easy to understand. When does God's providence and sovereignty abrogate our own choices? This was beyond Fadi's understanding. He can clearly see God's hand shape many events that took place in his life. He questioned whether it was God's will that guided the choices in his life, or whether his free will was the cause? And to what extent did God control his life. Was God simply guiding and prodding, or was he forcing the events? These were very tough questions that he did not yet feel he had an answer to. He trusted in God's love and benevolence. He prayed for guidance. He made his choices in the past without considering what God's will maybe concerning his choices. Now however, he prays and seeks God's will to be fulfilled in his life. He is a child of God now and he can speak to God freely, without fear. The distance between him and God was bridged by the cross of Jesus. Oh, how thankful he was for his redeemer and savior. He did not have to fear death and judgment anymore. He did not fear the tortures of the grave anymore. He finally understood that the nature of God is Love above all else. This was emancipating. He felt the heavy burden of fear, hate and revenge lifted from his heart. He felt truly free now. His emotions no longer controlled him, instead he had discipline over his emotions and desires such as he never had before. He understood that this was the work of the Holy Spirit.

In his former believes as a Moslem, he really never knew much about the Holy Spirit. He knew that Christians used the words: In the name of the Father, the Son and the Holy Spirit. But he never knew exactly what that meant. He often thought that Christians were "Mushrikeen" that they believed in three Gods, and not just one God as Moslems did. He knew that this was one of the strongest points of contention between Moslems and Christians. Yet he recalled that in the Quran it said that Jesus was born from the Virgin Mary, and that she was told by an angle that her 'would be child' was the word of God and a Spirit from him.

He also knew that according to Moslem believes; a fetus is not considered to be a living soul till God breathes into it a spirit on the

40th day. That is why abortion in Islam is allowed before the 40th day only and abortion is considered murder afterwards.

That was the extent of his knowledge regarding the Spirit of God. Now as a Christian however, he understands the significant role that the Spirit of God has in the life of the believer. The Spirit of God is the comforter and teacher that Jesus promised his followers. The Spirit of God that indwells all believers and gives them guidance and grace and strength. How blessed he felt to have the Spirit of God work in his life in such a loving way.

The Trinity which was so hard for him to imagine before had suddenly become central in his new believes, the way he conducted his life and his understanding of God.

In creation, God made Adam in his image. That does not mean that God looks like a man. If God is infinite in wisdom, power and presence, then he can't be limited by a physical shape. The finite dimensions of a human being don't apply to God. What that meant, Fadi understood, is that man too, was a trinity same as God.

Every person has a spirit, soul and body. One can't exist without the other or the person will die and cease to exist as a person. The spirit, soul and body are separate entities with separate characteristics, yet they are together one person.

One of his Christian friends told him once that the sun was an example of the Trinity. The sun has mass or matter, light and heat. The sun can't exist without any of these three elements, or it will cease to be a sun. A person can see the sunlight without feeling its warmth, or can feel its warmth without seeing its light. The light and warmth of the sun can be extended millions of miles away, yet separation of the three elements doesn't cause the sun to cease. Even when separated, the three elements remain as one. In the same way, God's word Jesus, left heaven and took the body of a man to redeem all of mankind. He understood that now and wished that he could tell all his Moslem brothers how much God loved them and that they don't need to fear the tortures of the grave or hell. That God's intentions towards mankind are good. That God so loved the world that he gave his only begotten son, that whosoever believes in him will not perish but have everlasting life.

Now that he was no longer afraid to ask questions, he was searching for answers on everything, from the nature of God to whether there were other creations on other planets. He knew that he would not find answers to everything but the fact that he could think and question without fear was so liberating to him and gave him a new sense of self worthiness and strength.

He and Hazem talked often and shared their thoughts. He was amazed at how much Hazem knew about different cultures and different religions. He found out that Hazem studied philosophy at the University of Beirut and that he wrote beautiful poetry. Hazem would share his poetry with Fadi as they walked the lonely roads together. One poem read as follows:

If all the stars,
In heaven above
Were filled with tears and sorrow,
And all the pain,
Of this world mundane
And fears of tomorrow
My heart will equal, then surpass
All that the stars can carry
For my pains cannot be measured
By earthly themes of worry
My heart is burdened by my sins
Countless since a child
Failures, doubt and rage within
With misery compiled
Where my God, can we meet

Is there a middle ground?
Where I could place
My sin and shame
Where mercy can be found
Who can take, your hand and mine
And put the two together
To make a covenant anew,
That will be bound and tethered
By a blood so clean and pure,
A blood of a living sacrifice
A lamb without a blemish, a cure
For sins of all to suffice
For God and Man to never more
Part in clear strife
And walk together along the shore
Of t' eternal river of life

They were already across the Chouf mountains and headed towards Zahle. They were stopped many times along the road by Shi'ite fighters and questioned. They were honest in their answers, and they were let go time after time. This was almost impossible at that time in Lebanon when being stopped by an opposing faction usually meant torture and death. They knew that their God was protecting them.

Zahle was known as the city of wine and poetry. It sits on the eastern foothills of Mt. Sannine. The Bardounin River almost bisects the center of the city. Many famous writers and poets were born in this city. It is a city of unique history and culture.

They spent several days in Zahle and enjoyed a somewhat peaceful time. This was an area under the control of the Syrian army and enjoyed relative peace at the time.

They found transportation from Zahle to Beirut in the form of an old microbus with another 20 or so travelers. Most of the travelers carried side arms. One of them had two hand grenades strapped to his belt. They had sandwiches of fried potatoes with slices of tomatoes and sumac rolled in large pieces of flat bread. Fadi loved fried eggplant sandwiches, but no eggplants were to be found in this season.

Fayroz was singing on the radio. Her angelic voice had a calming effect. Fadi listened to the songs while watching the scenery outside the window. It was a majestic site indeed. Hills and mountains rolled before his eyes. The ground was covered with new grass and poppy flowers. The sky was clear with a few white clouds. The sun was strong and warm. He felt rejuvenated. He turned to Hazem and saw him speaking to the person sitting next to him. He was an Armenian whose father was born in Aleppo and mother was born in Beirut. They spoke and laughed and seemed to be enjoying each other's company immensely. Hazem introduced him as Sarkis. He was a mechanic and had a shop in Beirut. During the war, his shop was bombed and looted several times. He finally closed his shop and started to deal with "imports"! He had family in Syria and would make regular trips there to buy cigarettes and perfumes then sell them in Beirut. He would come to Lebanon through Serghaya. He would pay several illegal tolls to Syrian soldiers, and they would let him bring things in. Despite the tolls he paid, he still made a decent profit.

They finally arrived in Beirut. The distance between the two cities was less than 40 Kilometers and should have taken little over an hour. Due to road conditions, it took them close to 3 hours. When they arrived in Beirut, they were tired and disheveled.

They said goodbye to their new friend and hailed a taxi. They gave the driver the address and he stepped on the gas pedal. The old Mercedes took off like a horse that was just poked by a pair of sharp spurs. Fadi and Hazem looked at each other and smiled. Nothing like driving in the streets of Beirut. The taxicab took suddenly to the left in order to pass another car. As the taxi sped up, a Peugeot sedan was coming head on in their direction. The driver kept on going forward till he was about 2 meters only from the Peugeot. The two cars started to swerve in opposite directions to avoid the impact. As they started to swerve, a motorcycle zoomed in between them among the curses and profanities of the two drivers.

Hazem and Fadi sat back and sighed. Yes, they were undoubtedly in Beirut now. It seemed to them that some things just never change…

They arrived at the address where Layla and her brother Filiep used to live. The building remained standing despite some large missing sections of the building. On the second floor, a large hole was seen, and through it a partially collapsed room could be seen. Fadi's heart almost stopped. That was the living room of Layla's apartment.

He ran upstairs followed by Hazem. The door to Layla's apartment was hanging by one hinge only. Broken glass was everywhere. Some old furniture was left in the apartment, but most everything else was looted. There was debris and broken glass everywhere.

Fadi saw some old red boots that Layla used to wear. He remembered how joyous she was last time she was wearing those boots. They were going together on a trip to Faraya to ski. He held the boots in his hands and started to cry. Hazem put his hand on his shoulder and told him: She may have left before all of this happened: "Let's ask around and see what we can find".

They went downstairs, but the apartment downstairs was in similar a shape with no one inside. They went to the building across the street. One of the occupants knew Layla and had seen Fadi visit her before. She told Fadi of Filiep's passing away and of Layla's immigration to "Amreeka". Fadi was relieved and saddened at the same time. He was happy that Layla was safe from all the troubles around. Sad for Filiep's death and loosing Layla.

He decided right there and then. He looked firmly at Hazem and told him that he was not going to lose Layla. He was going to find a way and follow her to America.

Chapter 29

Fahd was in the Nabatieh camp when the shelling started. He had been following Fadi for several days waiting for his chance to kill him. He had sworn that day that he will kill this Kafer no matter what. He made it his mission in life to track Fadi down and kill him. He saw Fadi and Hazem enter Abu Nidal's abode right before the shelling started. The camp was not new to him. His aunt lived there for many years. He grew up in a similar camp. He knew the people, the culture and the lingo. He immediately blended in with the refugees and waited for his chance. When the shelling started, he quickly got into a Jeep with some other fighters and headed to the front lines. He knew that his battle with the Israeli army would be different from his battle with the Kataeb. The Israelis were well equipped and trained and have been resisting this kind of guerilla warfare that the Palestinians were using for almost three decades.

He had gotten a hold of a Kalashnikov and some ammunition. As soon as he reached the edge of the camp all hell broke loose. There were shells exploding everywhere. Fire, smoke and dust filled the sky. People were dying and parts of bodies were flying everywhere.

He was not new to fighting, however. He ran as fast as he could behind the cover of rocks in order to get closer to the Israelis in hopes of possibly killing a few of them. Close behind him were two other fighters with similar intentions.

It was at least half an hour of running and hiding then running again till they saw the first line of tanks. They were immediately shocked by the awesome fire power that was displaced. They stood there looking at the advancing army breathlessly. There was nothing that they could do at all. It would be futile to fire at these tanks. They needed anti-tank missiles which they didn't have. Their only hope was to try and pick one or two soldiers who were advancing behind the tanks. They split a part to cover more ground and provide a harder target. Fahd quickly saw his opportunity when one of the tank commanders opened the top cover of the tank and his head and hands emerged from the tank. He was holding binoculars and was watching the battlefield. Fahd quickly pointed his weapon and fired. He was very quick and nervous when he fired and saw dust kick up from the side of the tank. He missed his target. He quickly ran to his left and dove behind a small elevation in the ground. He could not have done that any sooner. As soon as he hit dirt, the ground all around him was raised by the hundreds of bullets being sprayed from the tank. Rocks exploded as bullets hit them and small sharp pieces of rocks tore through the ground and the vegetation. Fahd felt something very sharp hit him in the right side somewhat to the back. He wasn't sure as to how bad the injury was and didn't have time to look. He kept on crawling on his hands and knees away from the tanks. He suddenly felt very nauseous and queasy. His right side became completely numb and he could no longer drag his right leg. He wasn't sure what was happening to him. He stopped crawling and looked down at his right side. A look of horror came into his eyes. His jacket was completely torn exposing his flesh. Blood was pouring from a deep open area in his side. He could see flesh and muscle inside the wound. He quickly regained his composure. He took off his Soloug and a handkerchief. He stuffed the handkerchief into the wound and wrapped the Soloug around his waist then pressed hard with his hand over the wound area. He was in deep anguish now. A strange coldness fell over his body. His efforts to stop the bleeding were not very successful. He saw fresh blood seep from between his fingers as he started to lose feeling in his hand. He lay down on his left side and looked at the sky. It was gray and dark. He couldn't see any clouds. How funny everything around him suddenly looked. It all seemed surreal. He started to smell a very strange odor coming from his own body. He did not know what it was. His eyes could no longer distinguish any forms, and everything became darker and darker slowly. He could hear sounds in the distance, but they meant nothing to him. He simply disregarded all sounds now except those of his own breath. He was breathing very slowly now. He did not want to lose this sound. It was the only thing in his environment now that he recognized. He felt very confused and terrified. Slowly, the sounds of his breath faded away and his body became ice cold and completely numb. He looked towards heaven one more time but all that he saw was utter darkness as he slipped away into oblivion.

Chapter · 30

Daoud was sickened by what he saw. He believed in the mission he carried out. The daily bombardment of northern Israeli towns must be stopped. Bombing refugee camps though was not to his taste. The hordes of people fleeing ahead of the Israeli tanks and making northward with what little they had was very disturbing to him. He was a builder, not a destroyer. His vision for Israel was that of a modern nation that can compete on the world stage in medical and technological innovations. A country that can be home to Jews from all over the world but can also give Palestinians a fair shake at equal participation in their own government, and fair treatment. He hoped for peaceful coexistence between Israel and its Arab neighbors. The events of these last few years took that hope away from him.

They say that history repeats itself, how true. How many endless wars and battles claimed this part of the world as host? How much blood was shed over this soil? How many cities were buried here never to see the sun again? He was certain that this is where history had started, and where it will end.

What troubled him the most was that most of what was happening was done in the name of God.

Jews, Christians and Moslems all claim to worship the same God, and all claim Abraham as their father. Jews make their claim through Isaac, Moslems through Ismael and Christians through faith. All believe that God promised the land of Canaan to Abraham. Yet

Abraham did not take the land by force. In fact, when Abraham came to Canaan, he bought whatever land he took from its inhabitants. First sign of trouble over the land did not occur with the inhabitants of the land who respected and loved Abraham and thought him to be a great man. It happened instead between Abraham and his nephew Lot over water rights. That was resolved by Abraham giving Lot choice of land. Trouble happened again when Abraham used Hager, his wife's servant, to get a child. His son Ismael, born from Hager, was his eldest son and his heir. When Sarah became pregnant with a child herself and gave birth to Isaac, the land could no longer hold Sarah and her son Isaac and Hager and her son Ismael together without strife. Abraham sent Hagar and Ismael away from Sarah and Isaac. The birth right was taken away from the elder son and given to the younger son Isaac.

The descendants of Isaac had to leave the land inherited from their patriarch Abraham and go to Egypt due to famine in the land. The story of how they were brought out of Egypt and led by Moses and Aaron and how they escaped the Pharaoh of Egypt is well known among believers of the Bible and the Quran. The Hebrews were led by Moses to the Promised Land, only he did not enter the Promised Land himself. Instead, Hebrew armies were led by Joshua into the Promised Land and forcibly removed its inhabitants by killing every man, woman and child and burning out their cities and villages. According to the Torah, they were supposed to cleanse and purify the land by destroying all presence of the pagan people who lived in it. This was ordered by Jehovah their God. Perhaps, this was the first act of genocide committed on that land.

The history of the Jewish people since then is well documented in the Old Testament part of the Bible and by other historians. Archeological digs and recorded history found in Egypt, Mesopotamia and Persia seem to verify most of the history written in the Bible.

A significant portion of that history involved wars between the Philistines and the Jews. The story of Samson and Delilah depicts the relationship between the two peoples and the distrust they had for each other. Only, in the days of Samson and Delilah, the philistines had the upper hand. The bitter war between King Saul and later on King David and the Philistines also depicted the hatred and long-lived animosity between them. The standoff between David and Goliath had become an allegory for the underdog worldwide. The Philistines of the Bible may have been depicted as Israel's worst enemies, yet their wars with the Israelites did not cause much loss of life in comparison to other wars. The Philistines themselves were invaders that came from the sea around the year 1175 BC and settled parts of the eastern coast of the Mediterranean Sea. They were settled mostly in five city states that were known as Gaza, Ashkelon, Akron, Ashdod and Gath. As a people they disappeared from the world stage of civilizations around 6th or 7th century before the birth of Jesus. They became mostly assimilated with the civilizations surrounding them.

The troubles of the Jewish people did not stop with the Philistines. The Assyrians proved to be even more vicious enemies. The Jews were taken into captivity to Babylon and the temple of Solomon destroyed around 600 BC. The Greeks led by Alexander the Great passed through Judea on their way to Egypt and conquered Gaza and Phoenicia around 330 BC. It was the Romans who did the most damage to the Jewish community in the few centuries to follow. Pompey the Great laid siege to and entered the temple around 63 BC. The Romans then occupied and ruled the land of Judea and Samaria. The Jewish revolt against Rome in 67-70 AD cost the loss of Jerusalem and the second temple as well as the loss of over 1,100,000 lives and the captivity and enslavement of over a 100,000 more Jews.

Over the centuries Jews were heavily persecuted by the Christians both in Europe as well as Byzantium. The rise of Islam and the invading Moslem armies and the fall of Byzantium into Moslem hands did not give the Jews any relief. They remained heavily persecuted by the Moslems, although they gained more freedom and rights particularly during the Golden Age of the Islamic Empire in Andalusia. Jewish scholars were respected, and Jewish culture grew during that age.

The expulsion of the Moslems from Spain and later, the start of the Spanish Inquisition brought misery to the Jews again. Persecution resumed intensely and culminated many centuries later in the systemic genocide of Jews in Germany and Eastern Europe.

Daoud was aware of the history of the Jewish people. He felt that the Jews needed a homeland where they are no longer persecuted. He did not like the way through which this home land was acquired though. He did not feel that Jews from all over the world had the right to come to a country that was not theirs and drive its inhabitants out by force and take over their lands and farms. Why did Jews feel that this was their God given right, he did not understand. As far as he knew, it was God that caused their expulsion from Judea and Israel in the first place.

Now that Israel exists and millions of Jews have migrated to the land and worked the land and rebuild it into a modern nation, he can't see how the Palestinians feel they have the right to drive Jews out. After all, where will they go? And who had a right to what they built?

He shook his head. How does one resolve such a situation? He can't see a fair solution no matter how hard he thought. The only thing that can be done now is for Jews and Palestinians to work with the international community and establish a peaceful compromise where restitution can be made to the Palestinians and a free separate Palestinian state can be established in the west bank. He felt that such a solution would be possible if religious zeal could be set aside. He knew better than to think that such a thing would happen, however. Religion is the air that Middle Eastern people breathe and is the water which they drink. It is part of every event and thought they have and every creed they practice.

He was tired of the conflict and of the war. Tired of life in this part of the world. He wanted to go someplace where his talents could be used for the betterment of people's lives. He had been thinking about this for a while now. Every time he thought about a place, his mind would take him to America. His uncle Paul lived in Chicago and had been in contact with him. He owned a construction company and needed help. Daoud could see himself in Chicago. It was a city where he could start a new life and build a legacy.

Chapter 31

Fadi arrived in Chicago in June of 1979. He did not know where Layla lived. Before leaving Lebanon, he was given an address of her relative in Chicago by some people who knew him. The address was wrong. He didn't know what to do. He was told that Albany Park had many Arab owned businesses where he could find work. He found a bakery on Lawrence Street and was given a job there. He worked at the bakery 60 hours a week and was paid 120 dollars per week for his toil. That was not much but was enough for the 100 dollars a month room next to the elevated railroad tracks that he rented from a Jordanian family.

He had to save some of his money in order to buy a car. Now he simply walked to work from where he lived. It took him about 50 minutes one way. He enjoyed walking to work greatly. He would spend the time singing and repeating Psalms and enjoying nature. He would pass by beggars occasionally and he would give generously despite his meager means.

In the bakery, he was ridiculed because of his faith. George, the owner of the bakery was a Lebanese and was a Christian by heritage. He was an atheist by choice. He loved gambling and drinking. He invited Fadi to go with him to a friend's house to gamble many times but Fadi would refuse. George made fun of Fadi and called him crazy. He would intentionally say dirty jokes whenever Fadi was present to embarrass and tease him.

Fadi worked very hard at the bakery and was by far the most productive worker. He did not take several breaks a day for smoking and did not waste time as the other workers did. He was well liked by all the customers due to his politeness and ever-present smile. Eventually George started to trust him above all other employees. After a while the teasing became less frequent and less insulting.

One day George called Fadi to the back room to have some tea together. They sat on some empty wooden crates and George started pouring the tea in the two cups. He told Fadi that he was very pleased with his work and was going to give him a raise. His weekly payment was going to increase by 30 dollars. Fadi was very happy with the news and thanked George. George further told him that he wanted to give him more responsibilities because he trusted him the most. George asked Fadi: What makes a young man like you cling to religion so much?

Fadi said: I love God and want to live my life according to his will. It has nothing to do with religion!

-What makes you believe so strongly in God? How do you know that he even exists? I believe that God is an invention of our minds.

-But what are we then and what is all this around us? How did all that come to be? Surely it was not invented by our minds!

-No, George replied. I believe that everything was here and then the first cells or plants were accidentally brought into existence by some accident of nature.

-If there is a universe, or an existence of planets and stars and living things, then there must be a beginning, a starting point. I believe that God is the beginning. That the light of creation burst from him and thus began the universe. I believe that his word which was spoken to create the universe is still creating an infinite number of universes.

-But then where did God come from?

-God is the beginning. Is there anything before the beginning?

-I must agree with you that there was a beginning. But what happened in time before God?

-George, you must understand that God is the beginning of all things including time. Time did not exist before God, nor was there a time when we can say God began. God is more infinite than time or space. Time and space are also his creation.

-You are confusing me Fadi. This is too much for me to think about. That is why I prefer not to believe that there is a God. It is easier that way. I think that life developed through evolution like Darwin said.

-Darwin doesn't address the beginning of life, but simply how life progressed through natural selection. Evolutionists believe that life began in the sea through some unexplained event that caused different chemicals to bind together forming the first amino acids. Then somehow these amino acids got together with compounds called bases and sugars, then formed very complex and well-organized DNA. Even the simple cell contains organelles and many different components that must be present together for the cell to survive. How did that first cell survive and learn how to get nutrients, then divide into more working cells? Believing in the accidental formation of life is like saying that a Swiss watch was accidently made from iron ore and other metals that somehow were refined and formed into the appropriate shapes and then sand accidently was heated and became glass that was shaped perfectly to fit the watch where all its pieces somehow jumped together and formed a working masterpiece. Do you see how foolish that idea is? Does it not make much more sense that a skilled watch maker made the watch?

-When you put it that way, I would have to agree with you. Truthfully, I suspect that deep in my heart I always believed in God, but I willfully reject the idea in my own mind. You see, believing in God means that I must answer to a higher authority for my actions. And I don't like to be subject to any authority but my own. I can't even stand the government. They burden us with taxes and laws. I like to be my own boss and responsible to myself only. Whenever God gets in the equation, I feel very guilty about all the bad thoughts and feelings and deeds that I have done. I just tell myself that everybody does the same. God can't put all of us into hell, and if he does, I am no better than everyone else.

Fadi laughed heartily and said: What makes you think that God's intentions towards mankind are so bad. God doesn't want anybody to go to hell. He loves us beyond anything you can imagine. The Bible says that God wants all people to be saved and to come to a knowledge of the truth.

-You see, that is where I have a problem. God wants all people to know the truth. Which truth is that? Everyone claims to know the truth. Jews believe that they are the only ones with the true knowledge of God. Moslems believe that their Prophet was the last of the prophets and that God's word was handed down to him in the form of the written Quran. Christians believe that Mohammad was a false prophet, and that Jesus was the Messiah that Jews were waiting for but rejected. Followers of these three religions have been killing each other for hundreds of years in the name of God. It is so messed up. This is why I hate religion.

-I agree with you that the world has suffered much at the hands of people who say they love God and are fighting for his cause. God however has nothing to do with man's foolishness. He did not ask us to kill each other for his sake. Anyone who believes that God is happy when people are killed for his name's sake, has no understanding whatsoever of God's nature. God invited people to love and serve each other to prove their love for him. The epistle of John, 4:20 says: Whoever claims to love God yet hates a brother or sister is a liar. For whoever does not love their brother and sister, whom they have seen, cannot love God, whom they have not seen. And when Jesus was asked as to which is the greatest commandment out of the Ten Commandments he replied: "'Love the Lord your God with all your heart and with all your soul and with all your mind. This is the first and greatest commandment. And the second is like it: 'Love your neighbor as yourself. All the Law and the Prophets hang on these two commandments'". Jesus also taught us to love even our enemies. He said: "But to you who are listening I say: Love your enemies, do good to those who hate you" This is why I placed my faith in Jesus. He did many miracles including raising the dead and healing the sick and blind. His greatest miracle though is how he changed our world and brought love and forgiveness and hope into it. George, if you want to know real happiness and peace, read the Bible. It will lead you to the true knowledge of God.

-Thank you Fadi for encouraging me. I feel so good after talking to you. I believe that I will take your advice and start reading the Bible...

Chapter 32

Layla had been working in an advertising agency owned by an Assyrian man named Eisho. He was a very short statured man with a very hairy face. His eyebrows looked like untrimmed thorn bushes. Long Hair was coming out of his ears and nostrils. His nose was long and crooked, and his lips were very thin. He was a cruel man. He hated paying out money despite the fact that his screen-printing business was doing very well. Layla tried to tolerate him. She would convince herself that underneath this obnoxious exterior there may be a decent person. On the other hand she could not explain away how especially cruel he seemed to treat her without any apparent reason.

She was doing art work and preparing the silk screens for him. He paid her for these efforts one hundred dollars weekly. Sometimes she would work till eight or nine o'clock in the evening to finish a project, but he would not pay her for the extra time.

What made her job tolerable was the presence of Samira. Samira was an Iraqi Assyrian girl who had been working for Eisho for eight years. She was a close friend of Eisho's wife Nahrain. Whenever Eisho became overbearing, she would talk to his wife. The next day he would always be nicer.

Samira soon became very close to Layla. She loved how sweet and gentle Layla was. She was very impressed by her talent and dedication. They often talked about the old country together and about how life was there. Layla was initially shy with Samira but was able to open to her as time passed and she felt that she could trust her more. She told her about her brother Phileip and how he died and told her about Aunt Rose and about Fadi.

Samira was very wise. She gave Layla great advice regarding work and regarding life in America. Layla loved listening to her. She would joke often with Layla and sometimes she would sing Assyrian songs with her very beautiful voice.

She told Layla where to go shopping and which areas to avoid. They went together several times to get Arabic foods and sweets from the shops on Lawrence Ave. and Kedzie Ave. where many Arab stores and restaurants were located.

It was on one of these shopping trips that Layla saw Fadi. She had just finished eating lunch with Samira at a Middle Eastern restaurant. They had Kebbeh and Falafel and stuffed grape leaves and were hardly able to move afterwards. Samira needed some spices and Pita bread, and they decided to walk to the bakery to work off some calories.

It was a pleasant sunny day. Layla felt very happy and rejuvenated. They were walking east on Lawrence Ave. and looking at all the shops. There were many ethnic shops along both sides of the street. Korean, Arabic and Indian shops were more abundant than others. There were people from all different countries present. She couldn't believe how diverse Chicago was. All these people and they seemed to live together mostly in harmony.

She heard about Chicago when she lived in Lebanon. How it was a vicious city filled with criminals and the Mafia. That there were shootings and bank robberies all the time. Since she came to Chicago however, she did not even see a single skirmish. She thought to herself why wouldn't people in the Middle East learn how to live with each other like people in America did?

They reached the bakery and went in. Layla had not been to this bakery before. She usually accompanied Elias and Fayrose to a different bakery on Devon Ave. The bakery shelves were filled with different types of canned foods and Middle Eastern imports. There were heaps of large rice bags and large cans of olive oil piled on top of each other in a large display. She saw the Pita bread on a rack close to the check-out counter. There were also sweets of different types displayed in a glass case and looked absolutely irresistible. A young man was standing behind the counter replenishing some supplies. He was wearing a red shirt and a pair of jeans and had a white hat on. He also had an apron wrapped around his waist. The cap along with his dense hair covered his face and hid his features.

Samira approached the counter and asked for the spices. Layla was not far from her. The young man behind the counter turned his head to Samira as he heard her request and started to point to the shelf where the spices are displayed. As he started to speak his face suddenly lost its color and his hand froze in mid-air. His mouth stayed open, and his lips started to tremble. His eyes shone suddenly as tears started to well up in the corners. He finally let his hand drop and whispered softly the word: Layla..

Layla looked up when she heard her name and saw Fadi. An overwhelming feeling of surprise and joy overcame her. She slapped her thighs with her hands as if to wake herself up and yelled: Fadi… Oh Fadi. My darling. I can't believe this is you. Hhhhow did you end up here. I had lost hope and thought that you were injured or even d…. Ya Habibi. Thank God you are safe.

She ran to him as he came around the counter and they hugged tightly. He started kissing her on her forehead and cheeks. She quickly pulled him by the shirt of his left arm and almost caused him to fall forward in her excitement to show him to Samira. She was laughing and hardly able to contain herself as she introduced him. Samira had never seen Layla this happy before and was almost jealous of her. She looked at

Fadi and scrutinized him carefully saying to herself: so, this is the man that won Layla's heart.

George came out from the back as he heard the commotion. Fadi immediately told him about Layla. George was happy to hear of Fadi's and Layla's reunion and told Fadi to take the rest of the day off and catch up with Layla.

In a minute Fadi took off his apron and hat and threw them behind the counter and ran outside holding Layla's hand and pulling her behind him. Samira followed quickly without buying her spices or bread. As the door closed behind her, George was standing behind the counter with a very broad smile on his face as a tear slowly fell down his left cheek.

Chapter 33

Daoud had just finished working out at the gym. He had recently met a young personal trainer there named Brendan. He started working out with him in order to get himself back in shape. Since he left the army, he had let himself go somewhat. He had started to gain weight and had lost the level of energy and stamina that he once had. Training with Brendan had been a blessing that he needed badly especially considering that he could talk to Brendan about a broad spectrum of subjects and get an intelligent conversation back from him.

Today was no different. They worked out together on stretching and conditioning, then used some power equipment for strengthening. They talked about what was happening in the Middle East while exercising. Brendan knew Daoud's background and often quizzed him on the meaning of different events in that part of the world.

Even though Daoud had left the IDF, he continued to be concerned with the state of his former country. He continued to consider himself and Israeli despite getting his American citizenship only a few weeks ago. He followed up on the news and was up to date on current events. He kept his contacts in the army and despite rigid security protocols, was able to keep up with inside news. He knew that Hizb Allah was becoming strong in Southern Lebanon and that Israel was getting ready for another incursion. The Syrian army had been slowly moving westward towards Beirut and Israel did not like what was happening. Behind the scenes negotiations with Hafez Assad the president of Syria were not fruitful at all.

After he left the gym, he went back to the construction site of a new shopping center being built. He was overseeing the project and was very attentive to the smallest of details. He ran a very tight ship but was fair to the workers and well respected by them. Two of the workers especially caught his attention. They were both middle eastern and one of them looked very familiar. They would work closely together, and he often saw them lunch together as well. He witnessed some very animated discussions between them during lunch hour. They would speak in Arabic and the shorter one of the two would often make angry faces and gestures while the quieter and taller one seemed much more composed and often had a smile on his face. He was the one that Daoud thought he recognized from somewhere in the past.

The two were very hard working. Despite their animated lunch discussions, they worked very well together. They seemed to give their full efforts daily and were also helpful to the rest of the crew. Daoud would laugh sometimes when he would see them offer to share what small lunch they had with others. He recognized these wonderful traits of Arabs, generosity and simplicity and willingness to help and share with others what they had. He stopped by them once when they were having lunch. They were having tea and eating some pita bread with olives, Labna (strained yogurt) and Hummus. He greeted them and they invited him for food. He sat down on some bags of cement with them and took a half pita and started to dip chunks of it into the Hummus and eat. They were very pleased to have him sit with them. They knew that he was the manager of the building project and felt honored that he sat with them and was sharing food with them. He asked them where they were from. The taller man was named Hazem. He was from Lebanon. The younger and shorter man was Muneer. He was from Yemen.

After that one time with Hazem and Muneer, Daoud stopped by occasionally to talk to them. Eventually he got to know both of them very well.

He recognized Hazem later as one of the two men that were helping the wounded in the Palestinian camp when it was overrun by Israeli troops. He did not say anything about that fact to Hazem. He did not want to bring the past back to life. He wanted to forget wars and war makers and wanted to do what he always wished for.... Build. He was a builder and not a destroyer. He had a philosophy that every person on earth should make whatever part of the world that person was living in better, prettier and happier. One should never leave a place as he found it. One should always leave it improved, no matter how small the improvement was.

On this day he went to his office first then at lunch time he brought out three cups, a thermos of hot tea and two dozen Falafel that he brought with him on his way in. He went to the back of the construction site where there was some shade and where Hazem and Muneer would usually have lunch. He found them there just starting their usual argument. They were talking about politics and religion. He smiled then greeted them. They both returned the greeting and were very happy to see him. They immediately put a clean towel on top of a box and started to put the pita bread and this time Foule (fava beans made with olive oil and parsley and lemon juice) They also had some onions and sliced tomatoes. Daoud put the Falafel on the makeshift table then he asked what the argument today was about.

Muneer was happy to volunteer an answer:

-Hazem was saying that Hizb Allah is an illegitimate group in Lebanon and that they should not be interfering with Lebanese politics. I think that they are a good counterbalance to the Southern Lebanese Army and to Israel's frequent incursions.

Daoud smiled again. He has heard these discussions thousands of times before. There is no gathering in the Middle East or among

Middle Eastern men that does not involve religion or politics. The issue of Israel must come up in every conversation.

Daoud said: I must agree with Hazem. Most of Hizb Allah fighters are not even Lebanese. This is no different than a foreign army occupation. They should not have been allowed to take over South Lebanon by the Lebanese army.

Hazem laughed and said: What army. The Lebanese army can't kick a fly out of Lebanon. Look at Syria and Israel. They go in and out of Lebanon any time they want. They do whatever they want. The Lebanese are busy killing each other. Lebanon is forever gone. I don't think that things will ever be the same again. Lebanon is now a divided country and will most likely remain so to the end of times.

Muneer commented: This is the way Amreeka and Israel want it to be. The more divided the Arabs are, the stronger and safer Israel is.

Daoud could only agree in his heart to what was said. He knew that the security of Israel depended in large part on weakening its neighbor states and preventing them from acting collectively.

They started to eat and drink tea then. Occasionally during lunch something would be said that would bring on a comment or a response. When lunch was finished, they had tea and started their discussion again. Lunch break here was an hour. It started at noon and ended at 1:00 pm. It gave the workers time to rest a little bit and for the hot noon sun to move west creating some shade and coolness.

Muneer said: I don't know why everybody fights Islam. We Moslems respect all the prophets and other religions. Why can't Christians and Jews accept our prophet and our book?

Hazem answered that Islam does not really accept other religions even though most Moslems think so. He said: How could Islam be accepting of other religions when the holy books of Islam describe Jews as Pigs and Monkeys and enemies of Allah and describe Christians as worshipers of three gods and as having counterfeited the Injeel (gospel). When the Quran says that Issa Ibn Mariam was not crucified and that he was only a prophet and not the incarnation of God then the Quran is attacking the foundations of Christian doctrine. We believe that God's sacrifice as Jesus on the cross and his resurrection are the only way for salvation. The Old Testament part of the Bible predicted the virgin birth of Jesus and his life, the way he would die and his resurrection. Over three hundred prophecies were fulfilled by Jesus.

Daoud pondered upon these words. He knew that what Christians called the Old Testament was the Jewish TaNaKh. A collection of the Torah, the Nivi'im (prophets) and Ketuvim (writings). Christians believed in these writings and included them in their Holy Bible. Moslems also had many stories and Jewish laws including the Ten Commandments as part of their belief system. He also wondered why the Moslems called their book Quran. From what he had heard, the word was not structurally sound according to the Arabic grammar and very closely resembled the Hebrew word "Miqra" which means "that which was read". That is exactly the meaning of the word Quran according to Moslems. He wondered how strong the link between the Quran and the Jewish and Christian writings was. He knew that the Quran was collected and assembled into several books and that the final copy of the Quran was canonized by Othman Ibn Affan around 656 AD. During that period, both the TaNaKh and the Christian Bible were already well established and translated into most of the languages of the world. All other copies of the Quran which differed in content from each other to some extent, were then ordered burned by Othman Ibn Affan. The final copy of the Quran was established in the Umayyad period around 750 AD, where the "Tashkil" (Diacritical points) were added to the Quran.

He was brought out of his reflective mode by the loud voice of Muneer saying that Moslems believe in Moses and in Issa. They believe in the Ten Commandments and in all the miracles that Issa performed and in his virgin birth. Why can't Christians and Jews be nice like Moslems and believe in Muhammad?

Hazem said: It is not about being nice. It is about where we will spend eternity and how we will live our lives here on earth. The truth must be sought after. Any person who wants to truly seek God must abandon all prejudice and pre-established thought and seek God whole-heartedly. No matter where his search may lead him, the person must be willing to sacrifice all for the true knowledge and worship of God.

These words struck Daoud to the core. They challenged his sense of who he really is. He was a Jew that did not really have much room in his life for God. Yet these two men followed the Christian and Moslem faith, both of which call Abraham a father and both of which owe their roots to Judaism and the God of Israel. Why can't he be truer to his own God?

His thoughts drifted again and the loud voices of Muneer and Hazem became more and more distant…

Chapter 34

Fadi and Layla started seeing each other almost every day. They became inseparable. Layla introduced him to Elias and Fayrose and he soon became close friends with both. They loved him for his strong faith and his integrity. They knew that he was genuinely in love with Layla and she was with him. Soon Layla and Fadi were married in New Life Church. Many of their friends were there with them. George and Samira were best man and maid of honor. The wedding was lovely and happy. The parishioners were delighted to have this new young couple added to their congregation. Everybody pitched in. People made Tabbouleh and Kibbeh and Baba Ghanoug and stuffed grape leaves and many other famous Lebanese dishes. It was a great feast. The best part of the feast was when a tall, dark young man stood at the end of one of the tables and toasted the new couple. Fadi was unable to hold back his tears when he saw the man and immediately recognized his friend Hazem. He looked at layla with tearful eyes and hugged her tightly. What was a perfect day for him was just made better by the presence of his friend.

Fadi had lost contact with Hazem after he came to Chicago. They were unable to keep up with each other due to rapidly changing contact numbers and inability to reach common friends in Lebanon. Many of their common friends relocated or were lost to the war and they completely lost contact from each other.

Hazem was able to immigrate to the United States with the help of the Catholic Church. He first went to Italy and stayed there for five months before his paperwork was completed, then he came to Chicago on an asylum visa. He chose Chicago due to more prevalent work opportunities and a large Arab population. He also knew that he would eventually find Fadi there.

He looked for Fadi many times but could not find him. He finally heard through a friend that attends New Life Church of the upcoming wedding and he was overjoyed upon hearing the names of the young couple. He went home that evening and knelt on his knees and praised and thanked God for his mercies and everlasting love. For his kindness to Fadi and Layla and for bringing them together again. He did not contact Fadi and wanted to surprise him. Indeed, it was a great and wonderful surprise. After the banquet they hugged each other and cried on each other's shoulders and made everyone around them cry. It was truly one of the happiest days at the church.

After Fadi and Layla went off to their honeymoon, Hazem went back to his apartment and spent the rest of the evening looking through some photographs that he had of Fadi and Layla. He remembered Aunt Rose and looked at some of her photographs as well. That night he cried and laughed for hours. The emotions were so strong and so many that he could not distinguish them apart.

He tried going to sleep but he couldn't. He read his Bible for a while then turned on some soft music and tried going to sleep again. He was not sure how long he tossed and turned before his phone rang. He answered the phone quickly and it was Muneer on the other line.

-What is going on Muneer? Are you alright?

-I couldn't fall asleep, and I was wondering if I could come over for some tea.

Hazem looked at his alarm clock and the time was 11:50 pm. He knew that they needed to wake up early in the morning to go to work, but he was unable to sleep, and he told Muneer to come over.

Muneer lived only a few blocks away. It must be something important that kept Muneer up that late. He was an early sleeper and rarely stayed up beyond 9:00 pm.

Muneer rang the doorbell and Hazem opened the door. He came in and Hazem saw the signs of alarm on his friend's face immediately. He invited him in and brought the tea pot and two cups over. He poured some sugar and tea into the cups. He made the tea while he was waiting for Muneer and had it ready for him when he arrived. As he poured the tea into the cups, steam came out. It was nice and hot and Muneer took his cup and sipped some tea immediately then sighed and looked at Hazem:

-I got a call from Yemen early today Hazem. My mother is very sick, and I was told that she may pass away at any moment. I don't know what to do. If I go back there, I may never be able to make it to the U.S again. I don't even have enough money saved up for a ticket and don't know if I could get one so soon anyway!

-I am so sorry to hear about your mother Muneer. I have some money saved up and can lend you what you need to buy a ticket. You need to act immediately, however. I will cover for you tomorrow at work and tell Daoud about what is happening. You need to see your mother if you can.

-I am afraid that I won't reach her in time. My brother said that she is in the hospital now and that the doctors told them that she may pass away at any moment. She had a massive stroke and seemed to be in a coma already. Even if I get there in time, I won't be able to talk to her. She won't even know that I am there. Oh, how much I wish that I never came here in the first place. I would have been at her side right now!

-Don't say that my friend. It was the will of God that brought you over here. God has good plans for your life. You have to trust him for that. Your mother would not want you to feel guilty about that. It was she that encouraged you to come to the U.S in the first place. She loves you greatly and wanted you to have a better life.

-I know that, but I still feel guilty for not being there right now. I have been calling out to God to spare her from death and to bring her out of the coma. I feel that my prayers are so small for such a great God and that the distance between us is so great. I don't know if he will even listen to me. I want you to pray for her Hazem! You seem to have so much faith in God. Please pray for her!

-My friend, I will be happy to pray for her, for you and all your family. You know that I care about you very much. As a matter of fact, you are in my prayers often.

-Really?! Why would you be praying for me often? We differ on so many things and we yell at each other all the time. I thought that you did not like the way I believe and that you were my enem…..

-I am not your enemy Muneer. I am your friend. I only have love and concern for you. We may disagree on the way we approach God and on many other things, but we are alike in one regard; we both seek God wholeheartedly. I know that one day you will have the peace with God that you are seeking and will no longer feel far from, but close to him. You will be able to pray to God in earnest trusting that he will not only hear, but also answer your prayers. Let's pray together for your mother right now. If it is God's will for her to live, she will come out of the coma, and you will see her again. Have faith my friend! Faith can move mountains!

-Thank you Hazem for not being offended by what I started to say. Fact is, I feel very close to you and respect you. I know that you are very close to God and that he listens to you. Please let's pray together.

They both knelt on their knees and lifted their heads up and started praying. It was almost morning when few strands of light started to come into Hazem's living room only to fall on two figures curled up on the floor snoring lightly with their hands still stretched forward…

Chapter 35

Fadi and Layla came back from their honeymoon feeling as if the whole world belonged to them. They were very happy and optimistic about their future together. Fadi wanted to quit the bakery and work somewhere else. He knew that the money he was making would not be enough for both and did not want to rely on Layla working in order to support them. He wanted her to have freedom to work only if she wanted to, but not feel that she needed to.

He called on Hazem and told him of his plans. Hazem immediately introduced him to Daoud. When Daoud and Fadi met to talk about the job, they both recognized each other immediately. Daoud smiled and said: So, we meet again. What a small world it is.

-It sure is a small world. Now I have a chance to thank you for sending us back some help on that day. You helped us save many lives.

Daoud smiled and answered: I am glad that I was of some help. At least we can look back at something good that we had done during that awful time.

Hazem was somewhat bewildered. He didn't understand what they were talking about and didn't know how they knew each other. He looked from one to the other back and forth listening to their dialogue. They finally looked at him smiling and Fadi asked Daoud:

-You never told him?

-Told me what? What is between you two? How do you know each other?

Daoud answered and told him where and how they have met in the past. On that dreadful day amidst the smoke and gunfire in Nabatea camp.

Hazem looked hard at Daoud then started to shake his head up and down as recognition came to his mind. He asked Daoud as to why he never told him and Daoud explained to him that he did not want him to feel uncomfortable working for a former Israeli soldier.

Hazem said: I no longer look at the world that way. I look at people and mostly see lost and lonely souls searching for answers to life and to different problems. Looking for inner peace and strength. Looking for stability and assurance. We are all alike. We have similar fears and aspirations and similar needs and wants. What most people differ in, is how they attempt to satisfy their needs. Some might look outside themselves and rely on family or friends. Others rely on their health and youth, strength or beauty. Others rely on money or power of position. Others rely on religion or superstition. Others like me rely on a most loving God. Some might consider that same as relying on religion. But I am not talking about religion which seems to separate people more than bring them together. We all saw that firsthand in Lebanon and still see it here in different ways. What I am talking about is a love relationship between God the creator and those he created. He made us with his own hands and breathed life into us from his own nostrils. He loves us despite all our transgressions. He gives us life and an abundance of gifts and blessings, yet only a few recognize him. He is the true source of all that is light and all that is pure and all that is good, yet people leave him who is the source of living and pure water and dig for themselves wells with murky waters to drink from. No Mr. Daoud, I would not have minded working for you if this is honest work.

-I am glad to hear that Hazem. You are one of my best workers and I truly enjoy talking to you and having lunch with you and with Muneer. By the way, how is Muneer now? How is he dealing with the death of his mother?

-He took her death very hard. We prayed for her together and we were hoping that God would give her more days to live. I guess that her appointed time was up and she had to leave this earth as we all have to someday. Muneer's only regret is that he didn't see her one more time before she died. He is happy that she was pleased with him and that he never angered her or went against her will. He was a very good son to her.

Fadi asked: Who is Muneer?

Hazem replied: He is a Yemeni who works with me. We are close friends.

Fadi asked Daoud if he could work for him. He told him that he would work very hard and that he is trying to build a life for himself and Layla and that Daoud would be pleased with his performance.

Daoud said: If you work as hard as I saw you that day in Nabatieh, I am sure that there will never be a problem between us. You can start working next Monday. Your pay will be same as Hazem even though he has been working here much longer. This is because you are married, and you have a young family to support now. Be a good and honest worker and you will have a good future with us.

-All I am asking for is a chance to prove myself.

-Very good then. See you on Monday.

Fadi thanked Daoud then went back with Hazem to his apartment. He cheerfully thanked his friend for all his help and told him that he would not disappoint him. He knew that Hazem put his reputation on the line to get him the job.

At the apartment Hazem fried some potatoes and eggplant while Fadi made some Hummus and tomato salad. They ate together and reminisced over old times for several hours. They were brothers in Christ and good friends and had shared many difficult memories together. Today, their companionship had given each of them renewed strength and resolve to live and succeed in this new country of theirs.

Chapter 36

Fadi proved himself to be a very hard worker indeed. He and Hazem and Muneer became well known in the company. They worked very well together and were entrusted with the most difficult tasks. Hazem was promoted into a supervisory position. That, however, did not stop the three from working very closely together still. Hazem was a hands-on type of supervisor and did more work than any of the men under him. He was very well liked by his crew.

Daoud remained close to the three Arabs and would have lunch and tea with them whenever circumstances permitted.

While Fadi was working in construction, Layla had taken courses at the community college and applied for a job as a bilingual teacher's aid. She was appointed at Roosevelt High School and started working in the bilingual department with Mrs. Yousef who taught English as a second language. She was happy with this job which took her away from home for part of the day and allowed her to interact with people from all nations. She loved working with the young men and women and was very liked by them herself. She was not much older than they were in chronological age, but it seemed as if she had already lived two lifetimes. She would often share some of her experiences in Lebanon with them and they would listen attentively. They respected her for her strength and faith and for being genuine.

In the evening Fadi would come home. They would cook dinner together and share in the cleaning of the dishes afterwards. They were very happy together. Prayer time and Bible study would come after dinner. It was a very precious time that brought them even closer to each other.

They often talked about their dreams and what they wanted to accomplish in life. Fadi wanted to continue doing construction work. It kept him in shape, and he enjoyed the challenge of working outside. He did not like working in the cold but enjoyed fighting against nature and being pushed to his physical limits. He told Layla he dreamed that one day he would participate in building the world's tallest building, and that he would be the one to put the finishing touches on the highest part of the building. Layla laughed when he told her that and said that he should start taking flying lessons right away. He needed to know how to fly in case the wind blew him away from the top.

He laughed at her comments and told her that he would do that if she agreed to take the lessons with him.

They were intensely in love and they were very happy. All the worries of the world seemed to be beneath them. No matter what difficulties they faced, they felt that together they can beat all obstacles. And obstacles they met time and time again.

Their first struggle was with the fact they Layla did not get pregnant. Despite trying for over two years, there was no pregnancy. Layla's doctor told them that she could see no apparent reason as to why they can't have children. They were both healthy and capable of having offspring. She gave Layla some vitamins and told her to continue trying.

They both loved kids and were yearning to hear a baby crying and laughing in their home. They fasted and prayed and asked God daily for the gift of a child, but God did not give them one.

Their lives then took a different turn. They never lost love for each other, but their joy was gone. They both felt abandoned by God. They couldn't understand why they were deprived of parenthood. They searched their hearts and lives for the presence of a sin that might have angered God. Fadi thought that he was being punished for all the people that he killed. Even though he repented, and he believed in God's forgiveness, these thoughts continued to torture him. He remembered the faces of the people that he killed. He would have nightmares about them and wake up in a sweat. He started to wake up late and go to work late. He lost his usual energy, and his friends noticed. Every time they asked him if there was a problem he would deny the presence of any.

Layla on the other hand became depressed and agitated. She blamed herself for the problem. She thought of herself as being less than whole. That she was not a normal woman. She cried daily. Her students noticed how she had changed and so had Mrs. Yousef. She asked her if there was a problem, but Layla could not discuss the particulars of her life with Mrs. Yousef. She did not know her well enough to discuss such private matters with her. But she had to turn to someone for help!

It was not long before she found the right person to open her heart to. She was sitting in the cafeteria during lunch break when she was approached by a well-dressed, tall and cheerful black lady. She introduced herself as Ora Lee Thompson, the art teacher. She was in her late fifties to early sixties Layla guessed. She sat next to Layla and told her that she had been watching her over the last two months and that she had been praying for her. Ora Lee told her:

-I used to see you in the corridors all the time and I sensed your sweet spirit. I have been praying for you since I saw you at the beginning of the school year. The last two months though, the Lord had put you in my heart and I've been praying for you in earnest. There is a problem in your life that the Lord is going to use for his glory. I know that you are suffering now, but your suffering is going to bring happiness and healing to many people. The Lord said that unless a grain of wheat dies and is buried in the soil it cannot bear fruit. We are like the grain of wheat honey; we can't flourish and bring fruit unless we forsake our own will and submit to the will of God.

Layla felt a great sense of peace talking to Ora Lee. She saw in her a very confident and tranquil person. Her demeanor seemed to be genuine and forthright. She spoke with elegance and compassion and Layla saw the love in her eyes as she spoke to her. She immediately trusted her. She put her head on Ora Lee's shoulder and cried silently. Ora Lee did not move a muscle. She just held her tight and waited. She did not speak to Layla till Layla finally stopped crying and lifted her head up and took a Kleenex from her purse and wiped away her tears.

Ora Lee looked at her compassionately and told her: You know that one day we won't need to wipe our tears away anymore. It will be God himself who will wipe away every tear from our eyes.

Layla lifted her head and smiled. The thought of God's hand gently wiping away her tears brought great comfort to her heart.

She thanked Ora Lee for her compassion then told her why she was crying. She wanted to have children with Fadi to feel that her life is complete and that she gave Fadi what he wanted most in life, a child.

-Sweetie, you can't blame yourself for that. It is God's will that you don't have a child yet. You must look beyond this need and see what God wants you to do with your life now. You can't keep waiting for things to happen. There are times when the door has already been opened for you to accomplish great things, but you don't accomplish anything because you won't step in. You wait for the door that you want to open. God's purpose for your life is much greater than you can envision. You must be still before God and allow him to reveal his will in your life to you!

-But I pray everyday Ora Lee! How else can I listen to God? What am I missing? I wish that I understood his will for my life more. I wish that I was like Aunt Rose. She was so peaceful all the time and so confident in her faith. She never seemed to falter. Even when her son was killed, she was peaceful with that. You know Ora Lee, you remind me a lot of her. I think that is why my heart opened to you immediately. Your presence has that same radiance and reassuring quality that she had. You make a person feel that they are in church just by sitting next to you.

Ora Lee laughed like a child that was just handed a piece of his or her favorite candy. She hugged Layla and told her that it was the presence of the Holy Spirit in her life. The closer we get to Jesus she said, the more we become like him. The fruits of the Holy Spirit are then revealed in our lives, thoughts and actions. The true measure of a Christian is not how often they go to church or how loudly they worship or what gifts they have. It is how much like Jesus they are.

Layla loved hearing Ora Lee speak. Her words brought Layla's mind back into focus. She indeed needed to get out of this self-pity mode and start thinking about what she wanted to accomplish through life, or rather, what God wanted to accomplish through her life….

Chapter 37

Fadi was working at a new construction site just south of downtown Chicago. Muneer was working with him. They were constructing the 45th floor of a new commercial building.

Fadi had been keeping to himself as of late. Despite Muneer's and Hazem's efforts to cheer him up and encourage him, he seemed to be getting worse every day.

Today was no different. He did his job well and did not allow himself any slack. He hardly spoke any words except those necessary to communicate with other workers what needed to be done. Hazem stopped by in the morning, but they did not converse much. Hazem gave instructions to the workers then went down to the office to give a report to Daoud. Muneer came over during lunch time to speak to Fadi.

Hi Fadi, so you continue to avoid me. Have I done something to upset you?

-No Muneer. You are a very good friend and a decent man. I am just depressed and want to be left alone for a while. I have many thoughts that I need to clear out.

-See what I mean. If you consider me a good friend, then you should be sharing these thoughts with me and allowing me to help you.

-Only God can help me with this problem Muneer. You know that we still don't have children. Every time I hear the laughter of a child or see a father walking with his son somewhere, I think of why I can't have a son or a daughter to carry or hug or walk with. I can't tell you how often I think about that. My life with Layla has been affected by it as well. We now avoid going to homes of friends who have children. She sees the pain in my eyes when I see a child and she blame herself for not giving me a child. She is not to blame. The doctor said that both of us can have kids. I don't know why we haven't yet. I feel as guilty as she does, and even more so for making her miserable. I don't know what to do Muneer. I have recently started thinking about adopting a child.

-Well, my friend, that may be what God wants you to do. There are many children without the fortune of having parents. You and Layla would make great parents and would provide a stable and a happy home to any child. Whatever child gets you two for parents is blessed by God. That child would live a very happy life, I am sure.

-Thank you Muneer. We may do just that. Who knows? Maybe we can adopt more than one child, and you are right, there are plenty of children in need of parents.

Tell me Muneer, how about you? Aren't you going to get married? What's holding you up for so long. You have a good job and you recently bought a small house. You should think about having a family!

-I am not ready for that yet. I have seen many marriages go down the drain and many men lose all that they worked so hard for all their lives due to divorce and family problems. I don't want to end up like that. I want to wait till I find a nice Arabian girl from a good Moslem family and get married to her.

-Can't you find someone from the Mosque? There must be many good families there.

-Moslem girls born in the United States are different than what you and I are used to. They want equal rights in everything. They want to work and have their own separate bank account and personal cars, and they are opinionated. I want a good old fashioned Moslem wife. One that listens to me and respects my will. One that I will find waiting for me when I get home with dinner on the table. One that will not ask to go shopping every other day. You know how we were raised. I want that type of life.

-I am afraid that you can't have that type of life here Muneer. Women here are liberated and have the same rights as men do. Even in Moslem families it is no different. The young ladies go to American schools and are exposed to American culture and learn from it.

-It is because Christian countries are loose with morals. Christian people don't care much about honor and chastity.

-You are utterly wrong Muneer. Jesus taught us that even looking at a woman the wrong way is considered adultery. We are taught to be modest and humble and pure. You can't judge an entire country by what you see on television and from a few people. Most Americans are conservative and godly people. Look at how much help Americans send to people all over the world.

-They send that money so that they can control their governments and politics. You think that the money that is being sent to Egypt by America is being sent there for the color of their eyes. It is to control them and bend their political will.

-Muneer, I am not talking about the American government here. I am talking about the American people. I have never seen a nation as charitable and as giving as America is. It is not the rich corporations or the big donations that empress me. It is the simple folks who have hardly enough to pay their own bills that give generously. They give to their churches, to charities, to neighbors in need and then send money overseas to help others. It may not be much, 10 dollars here, 20 dollars there. But it all adds up and shows you that the heart of

American people is in the right place. The American government plays politics with other countries and takes covert and sometimes ruthless actions against them. The government here in America seems to have lost its moral compass. It is infiltrated by lobbyists and special interest groups that buy with their money and power the votes of senators and affect the written laws of the land. It is infiltrated by Zionists that polarize the politics of the United States and cause this country to be alienated from many other countries. Instead of us being looked to as a beacon of hope, we are considered by many nations to be the epitome of colonialism.

-I am not sure that other governments are better anyway. Look at the Arab nations. You have all these dictators ruling their countries with an iron fist. They stay in power for thirty and forty years, then when they die, their sons take over leadership. No elections or respect to the will of the people, no challenging parties. All opposing political thoughts are outlawed and dissidents are tortured and executed. People are terrified of voicing their opinions. The slightest revolt is crushed ruthlessly by their armies and martial law takes effect. At least this country is ruled by a constitution. Even though powerful people seem to be able to find ways around obstacles all the time, yet the written law rules none the less.

-I agree with you Muneer. That is why we both came here in the first place isn't it? To be able to make something of our lives and leave a legacy for our children?

At the mention of the word children, Fadi's face darkened again, and his features changed. Muneer sensed that immediately and patted his friend on the shoulder.

-Let's go Fadi, it is time we got back to work. Inshalla (God willing) you will find you heart's desire soon.

They both got up and walked to the work zone. They had their lunch in a semi-finished space. In order to get to where they were working, they needed to cross some beams. They have gotten used to walking on these beams hundreds of feet above the ground without looking down. Their feet seemed to just know where to land. They had safety protocols that they followed. They all wore their construction hats and steel toed boots and had their support belts and clamps on. They would attach these clamps in their support belts to safety ropes and rails.

They walked safely to their work area and started to pick up their tools. As Fadi bent down to pick up his power riveter he heard a very loud clanging noise above him. He heard yelling and gasping and suddenly felt Muneer's rushing body impact him. He was immediately pushed several feet away as he watched to his horror a steel beam crash on Muneers head and upper body crushing him down. Muneer let out a loud sound and as his face hit the steel beneath him, his teeth were shattered and blood gushed from his nose and ears and mouth.

Fadi was in complete shock. Muneer had just pushed him out of the way to be crushed instead of him. He gave his life for him, and now he was laying on the steel floor silent with the heavy steel beam still over his body. There was no movement or sound coming out of him.

Fadi couldn't move at all. He was in complete shock. Other workers came to the site and lifted the beam off his body. Someone called the emergency response team. Paramedics arrived within minutes and carefully lifted Muneer up and placed him on a gurney. Fadi finally stood up and walked over to his friend's body. He was placed on his back. Paramedics had pronounced him dead on the scene. He put his hand over his friend's face and gently closed his wide-open eyes. All the other workers stood aside. The paramedic team gave Fadi some space. They could tell that there was camaraderie between these two workers. Fadi prayed over Muneer and cried loudly saying: You willingly gave your life for me. There is no greater love than this, that a man lays down his life for a friend. Thank you for your love and friendship. I will miss talking to you. I will miss your laughter and jokes. I will miss your arguments and strong opinions. You stood by me to the end and encouraged me in my times of desperation. A part of me will go with you my friend.

Daoud and Hazem arrived as Fadi was lamenting his friend's death. They heard an account of what happened from the men present. They both went over to Fadi and Muneer. Muneer's body was still warm. His face was bloodied and lips split. His nose was crushed, and a gaping hole was seen on the side of his skull. Daoud asked the paramedics to take the body to the hospital. Fadi wanted to accompany the body but was prevented from doing so by Daoud and Hazem. They took him downstairs and told him that he needed to see a counselor immediately to help him cope with what had just happened. Fadi refused to see a counselor and said that he just needs to go home to Layla and that he would need the next few days off. Daoud told him to take as much time off as he needed. Daoud left to the hospital to take care of all the legal arrangements while Hazem drove Fadi to his house. He half carried him to his bedroom. Fadi collapsed on his bed and started sobbing. Hazem took his work boots off him and let him lay there on his bed. After a few minutes Fadi became quiet. Hazem could see that Fadi went into slumber. He left him there and went out quietly and closed the bedroom door. He sat on the living room couch and started praying. He decided to wait for Layla and let her know of what events just took place. He prayed for Fadi and Layla, for Muneer and his family. He prayed for guidance for himself to know what to do for Muneer and how to find his relatives. As far as he knew, Muneer had no one in the United States. There were some Taxicab drivers from Yemen that knew him. He thought that he would go and see them tomorrow and see what he could find out. He knew that they hung out at a local café. He shook his head as he thought about Muneer and how many arguments they had together over religion and politics and social issues. They seemed to be on opposite ends almost all the time. Yet when time came and friendship was tested, Muneer did not hesitate to sacrifice his life for his friend. It was an automatic response. He did not think about religion or politics or social issues at the critical moment. Muneer instead acted instinctively out of love.

It was at least three or four hours before he heard the key turn into the lock at the front door. He must have slept himself as he was waiting for Layla. As Layla came into the room and saw Hazem, she smiled and welcomed him. She asked about Fadi and Hazem told her that Fadi was sleeping and that she should be quite and not wake him up. He told her about what happened and how Fadi was almost killed today was it not for the sacrifice of Muneer.

She sat down on the couch opposite him and was shaken to the core. She couldn't imagine life without Fadi. Her knees were shaken and her hands felt as if they were freezing. She got up immediately and made some hot tea. She thanked Hazem for bringing Fadi home. She started to inquire about Muneer's family and what they could do for them. She was indebted to Muneer for her husband's life. She wanted to do something to show her gratitude and to pay back for what he had done. Yet what could she do? And what payment would be enough for such a debt?

They had tea then Layla started to prepare dinner. She made some rice and baked chicken and went to wake Fadi up while Hazem was on the phone talking to Daoud to see what arrangements needed to be made. They needed to send Muneer's body to Yemen so that he could be buried there. They felt that since he has no family here, it would be best to do that. Muneer would have wanted it that way…

Chapter 38

It was two weeks after Muneer was killed. After his body was sent to his sister in Yemen that Daoud, Fadi and Hazem as well as many of the other construction workers and the owner of the company held a funeral for Muneer. Many of the workers came up and talked about him and about his honesty and how hard working he was.

It was Fadi's eulogy that made everybody tear up. He said:

I stand here today to speak about my departed friend Muneer. I am alive today because of his sacrifice. When that steel beam came tumbling down, he pushed me out of the way only to be crushed by the cold unforgiving steel himself. He did not only save my life by that act of love, but he also gave my life renewed purpose.

He was a Moslem friend. We had many similar beliefs but differed in faith on major issues. Despite our differences, we respected each other's beliefs and felt kinship with each other. We shared our thoughts together. We shared our dreams and fears together. We shared food and time together. We laughed and sometimes cried together. I will miss him terribly. I will miss him for the faithful friend that he is, and I will miss his companionship.

On the morning just before the accident, Muneer and I were talking together. I was feeling down and he came to cheer me up. I told him that the reason I was feeling down was because I did not have any children yet. I told him that I was thinking about adopting a child and he encouraged me to do so. He further said that there are many parentless children in this world and that the reason I don't have any children yet maybe because God wants me to take care of orphaned children instead.

My friend Muneer, you may not be here to hear me say this, but in tribute to you I announce that a long lived vision in my heart will start to break ground today. My wife Layla and I decided not to adopt a child of our own, but to establish an orphanage for children who were left destitute because of wars in the Middle East. The name of the orphanage will be called The Children of Abraham Orphanage. Christians, Moslems and Jews will all be welcomed to this orphanage. Maybe if they are raised together in an atmosphere of love and friendship, if they learn to respect each other and draw strength from each other's faith and devotion, then the cycle of hate and killing could be stopped. This may not occur by the establishment of one orphanage or the raising of one generation of friends but let this be a seed. A good seed that may turn into a large tree under which branches many circles of friendship may develop.

Thank you, my friend, for your love and sacrifice. It will not go in vain, and you will always be remembered.

After the funeral, Daoud and his uncle Paul came over to Fadi's house for dinner. Hazem also came there and brought Karen with him. She was a friend that he started to see on a regular basis lately. She was from his bible study group. She worked as an accountant and was single. They were thinking seriously about marriage. The accident with Muneer spoiled their plans to announce their intentions.

Daoud had also invited a very wealthy investor by the name of Martin Calgary. The invitation was made on a whim. It was right after the funeral service when Fadi announced his plans for the orphanage. Daoud had known Mr. Calgary through work associations and knew of his interests in charities for children. He had in the past supported such work in Ethiopia, India and Central Africa. Daoud thought that his expertise as well as his financial capabilities may be of tremendous help to Fadi's new plans.

Dinner was great. Layla made Tabbouleh, Kibbeh, Hummus and Bamieh. She also made Maqloubeh and sweets. The guests were stuffed by the end of dinner. Aromatic tea was made after dinner, and it was a great treat to all. The hot tea helped them digest the food and reinvigorated them.

They began discussing Fadi's plans afterwards. Fadi had been thinking about an orphanage since he was in Lebanon. He and Layla discussed that in the past many times, but it was always more of a dream that was never attempted. After Muneer's death, he decided to follow his heart and begin to build his dream. The orphanage offered him the opportunity to work with children whom he really loved and to do Christian Missions work which he also felt called for. Layla's teaching experience would come in handy as well. She would be responsible for developing the curriculum and for implementing the different educational and social programs. Hazem and Daoud offered to be on the board of directors. Karen offered to help with the financial aspects and bookkeeping of the orphanage.

What surprised all of them the most was the reaction of Paul, Daoud's uncle. He was known for his thriftiness and for not wanting to spend any money unless he absolutely needed to. This was a source of frustration for Daoud who always wanted to buy newer and better equipment. He would have to submit detailed studies and plans for each purchase, and it would take Paul several weeks to study it before approving or denying the request.

Today after hearing Fadi talk of his plans for an orphanage, he took Daoud aside and told him that he is interested in the project. He asked to go to Fadi's house with Daoud. When the discussion about the orphanage started after dinner, he announced that he is willing to contribute $250,000 towards the construction of the orphanage. Daoud was stunned by his uncle's announcement but welcomed it heartily and thought that this was a sign that God was blessing the project from the start.

Mr. Calgary announced that he would be willing to invest up to 2 million dollars over a period of five years in the project. He wanted one of his bookkeepers to have access to the books and be able to review the accounting periodically.

Fadi and Layla were very moved by all the support they received. They never thought that their dream can actually be fulfilled. Today, the soil was upturned, and the seeds were planted. There would be very hard work for them to do in the next few months especially. They needed to establish a legal structure for their ministry and needed to establish contacts in the Middle East with different faith groups in order to bring children over to the orphanage. They also needed to establish bylaws for the orphanage and a selection process for the children.

It was a new experience for both. They had many friends supporting them however and praying for them. New Life church which they attended in Palos Heights was a source of great help and inspiration to them as well. Pastors Freddie and Mary helped them with the establishment of the bylaws and some of the curriculum and were on the advisory board. Paula, Layla's best friend from church, was also a constant source of help and wisdom. She fervently prayed for the project and gave generously from her modest income. Her cheer, humble heart and abundant love gave Layla increased faith and energy. Together, they held a regular prayer meeting at church for the success of the project. Other church members contributed financially and with volunteering their time. Everyone was very excited about the project.

Fadi had to quit working construction to devote his time for his new ministry. He worked harder than any other time in his life to accomplish the work. Layla was also tireless in her efforts and her support of his work. Within the next 6 months they were able to establish and organize their team. They found a piece of property in North Chicago that was 25 acres. They bought the property and tore down the farm present on it and started to make plans for the buildings. Engineers from Paul's construction company did all the plans. His construction company also took on the project.

The actual construction took almost two years. When they were finished, they had a three-story dormitory and office building, a school, a cafeteria, a gym and a small medical clinic established on the property. The landscaping was beautiful and was another miracle. It was donated by an elderly Jewish lady from one of the local synagogues in North Chicago. She heard about the project and visited the site. After speaking to Fadi and Layla for a while, she took out her check book and wrote a check for fifty thousand dollars for landscaping purposes. A school bus was donated by a Moslem community from the Southside of Chicago. There were also individual donors from all backgrounds and faiths that donated for furniture and appliances and to the general fund.

At the end of two years the groundbreaking ceremony was held. All who participated in anyway were invited. Almost eight hundred people showed up to the opening ceremony. There were pastors, priests, rabbis and imams from different worship centers around the city. The mayor was present along with the state senator and other dignitaries. Most of the people who donated time and money, and labor were also there. It was the climax of the evening when Fadi pulled down the sheets covering the name of the orphanage at the entrance of the building. It read: Children Of Abraham Orphanage, above the writing was a white dove holding a green olive branch. There were shouts of joy and whistles and cheers and clapping of hands. Some people were overcome with emotion and started to cry. Among them was Layla and Ora Lee and Muneer's sister who was invited to the event and tickets and stay paid for by Fadi. It was indeed a night to remember.

Chapter 39

The next few years flew by very quickly. They were filled with challenges and events. Fadi and Layla worked very hard at the orphanage. In less than five years they had 200 children living there. They ranged in age from three years to fifteen years of age. There were boys and girls from all different areas of the Middle East and from all walks of life. Some came from wealthy families and had received good education, others came from refugee camps and had minimal to no education at all. The greatest challenge of all was to bring them all together and prevent them from getting segregated. They seemed to flock together according to nation and religion. This is exactly the barrier that Fadi and Layla wanted to break down. Violence was absolutely forbidden. There was a zero-tolerance policy to violence. All the kids were told that when they first arrived at the orphanage. Their education started immediately. They were placed in rooms that had kids with backgrounds different than their own. Immediately the more settled kids took them under their wings. Their days were well structured. They started their days with five minutes of reflection and prayer. They were allowed to pray in their own words and according to their faith. Morning exercises started after that. Different classes would then be held throughout the day. There were music and art classes as well as culture classes. Culture class was mandated to all students. The class offered studies on different cultural groups and had visitors from different cultures come in on a regular basis to expose the children to people from all over the world. A Tibetan monk was asked once to come and speak about the Tibetan culture. There was also a visitor from the Australian outback that spoke about his culture. Chinese, Russian, Polish, Irish, Norwegian, Red Indian, Brazilian, Egyptian, Syrian, Saudi, Nigerian... The list goes on and on. With all this exposure the children became very well aware of a global kinship that was present. They understood that people were very much alike no matter where they came from.

Some of the children later graduated from school and were sent to college on a scholarship. Few of them decided to become teachers and come back to the orphanage to teach there.

The Children of Abraham became a well- known and trusted institution. Other educational institutions came by and visited and looked at the curriculum and made changes to their own curriculum as a result.

Satellite orphanages were started in different countries after ten years. Daoud became head of overseas missions and personally oversaw the building of schools and medical clinics and orphanages on foreign soil in places like Bangladesh, Bolivia and Chad. He finally became the builder he always wanted to be.

Hazem became an Evangelist. He wanted to preach the love of Jesus to the whole world. He had a special place in his heart for his own people. He went back to Lebanon many times but was not well received there. He was beaten near to death twice. He was shot once, but the bullet only grazed his shoulder. He never gave up on his own people, however. He continued to organize yearly evangelistic events. Despite all the resistance, there were many souls that were won to Christ. He always quoted the Bible verse from Luke 15:7 " there will be more rejoicing in heaven over one sinner who repents than over ninety-nine righteous persons who do not need to repent." He would tell Fadi and Layla that a cat had nine lives, but he was a super cat and had eighteen. They would laugh warmly at that.

Layla continued to be Fadi's best friend and closest companion. They would sit together for hours at the end of the day and drink Mate'. They would talk about old times and old places. About their future goals and upcoming events. They enjoyed time with each other immensely.

They had all they wanted from life now. They did not feel the need for anything more except to see the name of their savior Jesus lifted up and praised. They wanted to serve him by loving the unloved and taking care of the forgotten. They did so passionately and tirelessly until the day that Fadi collapsed in his office after making his morning rounds. It was Elaine, his secretary that found him. She knocked on the door to bring him some paperwork to sign. He did not answer. She opened the door and found him on the floor hardly able to breathe. An ambulance was immediately called, and he was taken to the hospital. Layla immediately followed him there. She called Paula and Pastors Freddie and Mary and asked them to pray for Fadi.

At the hospital's emergency room Fadi was in a bed being treated. His condition had gotten better with the use of oxygen and pain medications. When she was finally allowed to speak to him, he told her that he was in the office going over some paperwork and suddenly felt that he could no longer breathe. He became lightheaded then fell to the floor. He reassured her that he was doing better now.

She was in a terrible state. She wanted to find out what happened to Fadi and asked to speak to his doctor. Dr. Shah came in and told her that they were not sure yet and that he would be sent to get a chest CT scan. Dr. Shah believed that Fadi may have had a pulmonary embolism. He asked her some questions about Fadi's previous health history and whether he was a smoker or not. She answered all his questions and was talking to him when transport came in to take Fadi to Radiology. She waited for him in the room for about half an hour. When he came back, he was feeling tired. She started stroking his hair and kissing him. She told him that everything would be better.

He went to sleep feeling safe at the touch of her hands. It was almost an hour later that Dr. Shah came in and told her …

Chapter 40

Layla came to Fadi's room early. He had just had another treatment and was feeling very sick. The site of Layla brought life back to his tired eyes. He straightened up and asked her about the orphanage. She said that all was well and that everything was being handled appropriately. They had many trustworthy people working there and the children themselves were on their best behavior for him not to worry. Everyone was praying for him. Layla told him how often she would be stopped in the corridor by the children and be asked about him and about his health. She told him that everyone missed him.

Fadi said that he missed all of them as well. He was proud of all of them. He asked Layla to tell them that when she went back.

-You will tell them yourself when you leave here Habibi. They don't want to hear it from me. They want to hear it from the horse's mouth.

-So am a horse now hah? Thank you honey

-You know what I mean, stop horsing around and tell me, how was your treatment session today?

-As usual. I would not wish this onto anyone. I really think that I should just go home now and let whatever God has in plan for me take place. I want to be home with you when the Lord asks for me.

-Please don't say that anymore Fadi. You have always been a fighter. Don't quit on me now.

-I have lived a full life. God was merciful enough to me to let me atone for some of my sins. I couldn't have dreamed of doing so much with the orphanage as has been done. And to remember that there was a day when I caused children to lose their fathers. Oh, every time I remember those days I get sick with regret. Thank God for second chances.

-The whole country was insane in those days Fadi. But we are beyond all of that now. Look at how much we accomplished together. We made a great team Habibi and it is not time yet to break up the team.

-You know very well that it is not our decision in the first place. When the appointed time comes, I will go. You will follow me there. There is no need to be sad. Life is very short indeed no matter how many years we live. What is the short time we live on earth in comparison to eternity. I am happy that I will be waiting for you in heaven. There, we won't remember the bad times anymore. We won't have regrets, and we won't feel pain.

Daoud and Hazem walked into the room as Fadi was speaking and Layla turned her head towards them and smiled. They came close to Fadi's bed, but he continued to speak. His eyes seemed fixated above and his face was radiant. A wide smile was on his face. He tightened his grip on Layla's hand and continued to say:

The angel showed me the river of the water of life, as clear as crystal, flowing from the throne of God and of the Lamb down the middle of the great street of the city. On each side of the river stood the tree of life, bearing twelve crops of fruit, yielding its fruit every month. And the leaves of the tree are for the healing of the nations. No longer will there be any curse. The throne of God and of the Lamb will be in the city, and his servants will serve him. They will see his face, and his name will be on their foreheads. There will be no more night. They will not need the light of a lamp or the light of the sun, for the Lord God will give them light. And they will reign for ever and ever.

Layla, Hazem and Daoud were standing by his side listening to him. They have read this passage in the book of revelation and now as Fadi recited it, they better understood the significance of these encouraging scriptures. These were not mere words, but a promise that they will be with God and with other believers once the journey here is finished. That no matter how destitute life may leave them, they will not be orphaned. That they have a heavenly father waiting for them and they have an eternal home. A home where there is no strife, no hatred, no evil and no wars. A place where the children of Abraham will come together from all the nations of the world to live forever with their loving God.

9 798889 391367 5